BIGFOOT BLOOD FRENZY

SAM M. PHILLIPS

SEVEREDPRESS

BIGFOOT BLOOD FRENZY

Copyright © 2025 by Sam M. Phillips

WWW.SEVEREDPRESS.COM

ISBN: 978-1-923165-67-0

1

Silver nimbus halos wreathed the contours of the night sky, mirroring the soft shadowy light of the wooden mountains below. A whispered wind spoke ominously in the trees, a rustling warning signal which made the animals of the forest hunch low, eyes wide, ears pricked. The luminous clouds above said nothing as they sped towards the horizon, able to flee and not wanting to witness the coming scene of carnage.

For us there was no such means of escape. Forced to live through the nightmare, we could only watch as the blood flowed and the corpses piled up.

***

A word written in black ink like a signature on a death sentence: Nightcap.

Luna frowned at it as she looked at the map again, folding and unfolding it like an origami paper fortune teller they'd made as children.

You're not a child anymore.

The thought rang in her mind as she twisted the map in her hands, lifting a flap of paper to reveal what was beneath. That word again—Nightcap. She closed the flap like a slammed door, frustrated, and put her fingers in what felt like the right places, singing her way through the count of a nursery rhyme as she worked the fortune teller.

Stop it. Damn this OCD.

Her fingers shook as she finished the rhyme again—it wouldn't be the last time.

Why are you scared?

She could feel the judgement, even if it mainly radiated from herself, rather than from her nearby partner. Sol held his tongue, though she could hear his thoughts, knew he was trying to be patient. The patience was fading fast.

Because we're lost.

She tried to focus, tried to count, to remember she'd already done this before and not to doubt herself.

The definition of insanity is what, again?

If she picked the right number, orientated the folded map right, they would find a way out of this mess. Revealed this time—or the time after—would be a grid number, a compass bearing, the distance from here to safety. She would see something she would recognise and *remember*. She'd be certain.

Sol reached a hand over her shoulder, took the confused mess of folded paper out of her hands. Her jumbled thoughts went with it like a puff of smoke, and she was left dazed and confused. With a certainty which infuriated Luna, he flattened all the creases she had made, laid the map out on a rock, took the whole picture in at once.

"We're not going to be able to figure it out without eyeballing a landmark," he said.

Luna hopped from one foot to the other like a curious bird, edgy to get going. She turned in a circle, trying to see something, anything.

"Just trees," she said, shoulders slumping in defeat.

"And the track," said Sol, stabbing a finger at the map. Luna leant forward to look.

"How can you be sure that's the track we're on?" she asked.

"I'm not sure. It's a guess."

"Then you're no better than me."

"I never said I was."

"At least I admit I don't know which way to go."

"We're lost, are you happy?" said Sol, throwing his hands in the air.

Luna scrunched up her face like a bunched fist.

I never feel happy anymore.

"No," she said.

"Well, neither am I, alright? We'll just have to camp here for the night and figure it out in the morning."

Luna's face further distorted in disgust. "But this isn't a campsite."

She kicked petulantly at the ground. It was a dirt track hemmed in by tall trees. They loomed over them like ominous sentinels, their branches spikey weapons pointed inwards, not admitting passage through to the dense forest beyond. The only way out was the track, and it twisted off into a black hole like a noose threaded through a gallows, disappearing into darkness as if through a trapdoor. Luna shuddered.

"We keep walking around in the dark we're going to fall off a cliff or something," said Sol.

"Yeah, I get that. But here?"

"One place is as good as the next right now. We've got a tent, food, water. What else could you need?"

Luna could think of many things. She kept her mouth shut, but her thoughts raced on.

Why did I let him drag me out here on this hiking trip?

Sol dropped his pack, helped Luna take off hers. The burden released, she felt a bit lighter, but really the weight only shifted forward, down into her gut, and hung there like a lump, a feeling of dread which settled in to stay, promising to ruin both their lives.

"I don't feel so great," she said.

Sol handed her a bottle. "Here, have some water, you big baby."

"Big?" she pouted.

Sol rolled his eyes, unrolled the tent. Luna tried to help set it up. She got the poles put together, but did it wrong. Sol had to undo what she had done. Annoyed with herself, she picked up the map and folded it again, singing and asking the fortune teller a silent question.

Why am I so hopeless?

"Care for a nightcap?" asked Sol, producing a bottle of whiskey as they got into the erected tent.

Luna shook her head, focused on her ritual. "I feel like that's what got us into this mess in the first place."

She lifted a flap of paper, sure of what she would find written there.

2

Nightcap—the word floated in Luna's dreams like a mirage as she slept. She knew it was the name of a mountain—or a range of mountains—and that there was an associated national park in which they hiked. But whether this was located in her native Australia or Sol's California wasn't clear in her dreamscape. She was as lost here as in waking life.

In a way she inhabited both locations, Australia and America mirroring each other, forming a dichotomous relationship just as Luna and Sol did themselves. Northern Hemisphere, Southern Hemisphere, and the same for east and west—polar opposites, one the shadow of the other, a bright light and a dim moon glow, waxing and waning in turn so that it was never clear who was in the ascendant.

But even this was an illusion. There was no winner, no ruler, only co-operation, love.

There is no shadow without light, no light without shadow.

Luna felt she had no form without Sol, no reason to be. In the same way, Sol was given boundaries by her, and though she felt guilty to drag him down like this, to contain him, she knew that without her he would have no vessel, no way to manifest.

The lump in her gut flipped over, demanding attention. Bile rose in her throat, waking her with a violent projection of matter. She barely made it to the tent flap to vomit onto the dirt.

The sun was rising in the east, its light reflecting on the patch of vomit, making it real. Luna crinkled her nose at the stench of consequences and turned away from it.

***

"Did you know Nightcap is actually a corruption of the original name, which was Night Camp," said Sol, smiling as he packed up the tent, the sun gleaming on his perfect teeth.

"You seem chipper this morning," said Luna, feeling fat and ugly. She didn't help with the tent, because to pack up meant they were one step closer to facing something she didn't want to face.

"What's the matter?" asked Sol, doing the job better without her anyway.

"I told you, I'm not well."

"Oh, right, the vomit. You didn't even drink anything last night."

Luna's expression soured. She placed a hand on her stomach. "I must have eaten something bad."

"We've only got these dehydrated ration packs."

"I feel like a dehydrated ration pack."

"What's eating you?"

Luna huffed, looked down at her body.

A damned parasite.

"You're a leech, you know that?" she said to Sol.

Sol was in the process of transferring some of the weight of supplies from Luna's pack to his own to lighten her load. "Wait, I'm what?"

She turned away. "Nothing."

"How am I a leech?" He took even more out of her pack, loading his own up further.

"Look, I don't have a lot to give," she said. "I feel like you're asking a lot of me, dragging me out here on this hike. And now we're lost and I don't know what to do."

"I'll look after you."

Luna shook her head.

Maybe now you will, but what about later? You'll run away like the rest of them.

"I'm not going to abandon you," said Sol, as if reading her thoughts.

"Yeah, because then the police will show up at your place asking questions," she deadpanned as she stood up. She laid a hand on her pack to stop him taking anything else out of it.

I can carry my own weight, thank you very much.

She started singing again to drown out her thoughts, running through the nursery rhyme and counting compulsively. Her thoughts wouldn't be silent though, overlapping like a round sung by multiple voices.

I carry that and so much more. A burden of the future, waiting to destroy both our lives even as it promises a fresh dawn. But even the light is an illusion, and Sol's blind optimism makes me nauseous.

Luna doubled over and vomited again.

I can't trust him any more than I trust myself.

3

Luna was horrified as Sol took them on the path which led up into the mountains. The trees seemed to be getting thicker, closing in on both sides like cattle gates, herding them towards the slaughter.

"Why are we going deeper into the forest?" she asked him. Even with the lighter of the two packs she felt she was going to keel over. The sun was slicing down on the exposed path. She was burning up.

Damn trees can't even provide shade.

"I told you already," said Sol, exasperated. "We have to find a vantage point so I can locate some landmarks and take a few bearings. Then I can triangulate our position and we're no longer lost."

"But with further to walk out. Why don't we go downhill?"

"The easy way isn't always the right way. We could die out here, you know?"

"Great, some date you've brought me on."

"It was meant to be a fun adventure."

"Not everything in life is a fun adventure."

"I feel like I should be saying that to you."

"And what's that supposed to mean?"

"For you, if something's hard, it's not worth doing."

"You think my life is easy," said Luna.

One, two, three, four…

"You have your struggles, but you make them harder than they have to be," said Sol.

"You know nothing about it. Give me the map."

"What, so you can do more OCD? We need the map. I'm using it. You'll wear it out from folding it over and over with your schoolyard nonsense."

"See? You think I'm making it up. It's a real problem. I have a diagnosis."

"I know you have a real problem. But you never do anything about it. When are you going to see you need to be on medication?"

"I need to see the map!" snapped Luna, stomping her foot.

"Or what?"

"Or we'll die, of course," said Luna.

It's that serious. It always is. The rituals are a matter of life or death.

"I'm just saying, with the right medication, it could ease your suffering," said Sol.

"You mean annoy you less." She snatched at the pouch at Sol's waist, opening the waterproof flap. "Give me the map."

"You're tearing it," said Sol, fighting with her as she got hold of the map. "We need it in one piece to get home."

Luna shrieked, her thoughts razor blades, cutting her.

My soul is being ripped in half. I can't decide what to do, which way to turn. I'm lost.

"Look what you've done," said Sol, half in fury, half in despair.

Luna looked down at the shredded scraps of paper she held, with their disconnected trails and severed contour lines crisscrossing patchwork scraps of white and green. There was only a single piece of map large enough to still contain a full word.

"Nightcap," she read for a final time, feeling a blissful release from the burden of needing to repeat her ritual. She threw the confetti—made of what had once been their only guide—into the air, and spun, arms out, like a child in the snow, as it rained down. She was free at last, if only for a moment.

***

The word Nightcap drifted away, floating on the air in the same way the tops of the mountains of the range seemed to as clouds gathered around their bases, disconnecting them from the earth, from reality. Into this dreamy space—where imagination mingled with human dread to create nightmares— was born a creature of myth, given life by the subconscious mind, where fear reigned and darkness was given form.

And this was not to say that the creature was not real, only that it was now made perceivable to human thought and sight where before it had been invisible. Terror bridged the gap. Luna's tattered sanity created the hole through which it could tread. Yet the creature was independent of those who perceived its coming. It had a life of its own, ambitions of its own, and a cycle of rebirth it was chained to in the mortal realm—just like mankind. It also had a name.

Bigfoot.

As it stomped through the forest, the trees parting for their master, the scrap of paper from the map landed on its hulking shoulder like a fleck of ash falling from a bushfire. The creature brushed it away as easily as it would brush away human life. Nothing would stand in the way of its own survival in this harsh world, nor its propagation as a species, however rare and supposedly ephemeral it was.

To it, what was real was flesh and blood.

4

"I'm sorry, I don't know what's gotten into me," said Luna, sitting down, exhaustion weighing on her, her energy all tied up in jangling neurons, lightning bolts playing around on the inside of her skull. "My hormones are all over the shop."

"It's not hormones," said Sol. "You're not mentally well. You know the solution, and yet you refuse to do anything about it."

Luna started to cry.

I'm trapped. I have no way out.

"Stop that," said Sol, dropping his pack. He fished out the whiskey bottle.

"That's your solution to everything," said Luna through tears. She looked up and down the trail. Both ways looked identical, providing no choice at all.

"It's not for me. It's for you, to calm you down," said Sol.

"Sedate me, you mean," sobbed Luna, "just like the medication. Then you don't have to deal with me."

"I deal with you plenty."

"So that's it. I'm a burden to you."

"You are right now. You tore up the fucking map."

Luna covered her ears, rocked back and forth. "Don't shout at me."

"I'm not."

"You're swearing."

"I'm fucking angry."

"Well, so am I."

"A moment ago you were frantic to get hold of the map. Then when you got it you were happy for all of four seconds. Next moment you're on the ground crying. Now you say you're angry."

"I told you, my hormones."

"Take a drink."

Luna shook her head. "I can't."

Sol took a step back, as if recoiling in disgust. He looked at her askance. "You're not pregnant, are you?"

"What? No."

Yes.

"Maybe you've got your period," suggested Sol. He sniffed the air like a bloodhound searching for a scent. Luna made a face.

I definitely don't.

"We've got no choice but to go on," said Sol, practical as ever, brushing over the other matter. Luna wished she could compartmentalise that easily.

Neat little boxes, all life's problems with their own space, each containing a poison snake of mental illness, ready to spring out—you're not immune to them, Sol, you only ignore them. But what we fear is out there, even if we pay it no mind.

"I'm scared," she said, the only summary of her thoughts she could come up with, wanting him to fill in the blanks, take care of the empty spaces in her mind by packing them full of reassurances.

It's just the OCD. It's just the OCD. It's just the OCD. One, two, three.

"It's natural to be scared," said Sol. "We're lost in the woods. But you've got to get a hold of yourself."

"Hold me," said Luna, getting up and extending her arms for a hug he didn't reciprocate. She wrapped him up, held him how she wanted to be held. It didn't stop her nerves from jangling around her body. Her thoughts were a blocked drain, filling up with dirty water.

One, two, three. One, two, three.

Even if she could unblock them, they would only swirl around, twirling her like a partner in a dance, leading her in the steps which must be taken, rather than the ones she would choose. She took a few halting steps down one direction of the path, then turned, went the other way. Both seemed so identical, the distances just numbers, counting down to a doom which felt inevitable, with no choices to be made, only plot points in a story, leading towards an ending she was not writing for herself.

I don't want this baby.

"We'll do this together," said Sol, belatedly taking her hand and leading her along.

She pulled her hand free. "You don't know the way any better than I do."

"But we can still get to high ground. Maybe from there we can see which way to head. We'll see a building, or some smoke, or even the ocean, maybe."

Luna frowned, trying hard to remember, and then said with certainty, "The Pacific Ocean."

But looking at it from east or west?

She fished a compact mirror out of a pocket, looked at herself. She didn't recognise the reflection, the face a mask of horror, showing her another side of a reality she didn't want to look at. She caught a glimpse of something large and hairy looming over her shoulder. She spun, gasping in fright—it was just Sol, his long hair matted with sweat, his beard unkempt.

"You look like someone else," Luna said to him, or to herself. But an image of another face loomed in her subconscious like an afterimage left by staring at the sun.

Sol smiled. But Luna saw only the dark side of the moon, an unfriendly smile beaming out into space, something never seen by human eyes, only glimpsed in dreams.

In her waking nightmare she witnessed the face of the monster and recoiled.

But there was nowhere to run, only a mountain to climb with the hope of seeing clearer at the top of it.

5

As they ascended the mountain they were wreathed in a mourning veil of grey gossamer cloth, fog closing in to smother them. It seemed as if they were passing from the real world into a spiritual realm, with only the burning promise of a bright dot up ahead, a beacon to draw them on. But was this light warning them away from the rocks, or drawing them onto their jagged edges? They could do nothing but follow it upwards, their only source of navigation as the trail disappeared beneath their feet.

The mountain became more treacherous, the climbing difficult. The trees melted away, turning to stone as if petrified by human touch. Neither Sol nor Luna spoke, both afraid to break the eerie silence which clutched their throats like the hands of a killer.

With relief they broke through the dense fog into the open air at the summit. It was like breaching the surface of the ocean after being held under, and they gasped at the sense of life-giving freedom and space. Smiles broke upon their faces but then were shattered as if under a hammer blow, teeth disappearing into sagging flesh as their mouths turned down. Their elation at having conquered the mountain was inverted, becoming a pit of despair.

They couldn't see a thing.

The fog formed an obscuring blanket which covered the earth like dirty wool. The sky overhead was steel grey, with no features apart from the sun sinking into a soft horizon. A haze settled on Sol and Luna's hearts, making even their own feelings unclear.

"At least we know which way is west," said Sol, pointing at the flattening smear of yellow that was the setting sun.

Luna swung her arms around in a circle. "And what good is a direction when you don't know where it leads?" she said, and turned her back in disgust, descending down into the fog once more. The greyness closed on top of her like a coffin lid as the last rays of the sun were snuffed out like a candle.

***

They shambled through the night like zombies, too afraid to stop, too weary to care. Each carried their personal burdens in solitude, isolated from the other even by small distances in the inky darkness, the moon similarly hidden behind its thick veil of clouds.

To Luna, Sol was as opaque as the night, usually so chatty, now reduced to shuffling steps as the only articulation of his existence. They couldn't even see if they were leaving footprints in the dirt track. She put a hand on her stomach.

Who will follow us?

"Someone will come looking," said Sol finally, his words bursting upon her like a sudden dawn. But it was a false light, one easily quenched in the tempering waters of reason.

"Come looking where?" asked Luna. "We don't even know where we are."

"We should stop and make camp. We're getting more lost pushing on like this."

"How do we get more lost?"

"Let's just stop," he said, groping for her in the dark. His fingers felt cold and rigor mortis stiff—the hands of the dead. Their touch made Luna shiver. The fingers looped around her wrists like handcuffs, and Luna felt like a condemned criminal being led to the gallows. She could hear the heavy footfalls of fate beating like a heart in her ears. Only she wasn't moving, and neither was Sol.

"What is that?" she hissed in Sol's ear, pulling him close like a human shield.

He instinctively recoiled, untangled himself from her grasping arms. "Why are you whispering?"

"Shut up, don't you hear it?"

But the noise had stopped.

"It's probably just an animal in the trees," he said.

"I'm scared, Sol."

"Whatever it is, it's more afraid of you than of us." His calmness made him sound condescending.

"It couldn't possibly be more afraid of me than I am of it. It's not a bloody spider," she said.

A single footstep pounded the ground like the reverberating note of a drum.

"Uh…" said Sol, "that was a rock coming loose from up the mountain."

"You sure?"

"I'm sure." He didn't sound it.

"What knocked it loose?"

"The wind?"

The trees rustled, something passing through the branches.

"And what was that?" she asked.

He let out a breath he must have been holding. "That was definitely the wind."

Luna could hear the smile in his voice. Her own lips twisted into a grimace at a new sound. A moan like that of a ghost swirled around them, echoing through the forest. The warbling note bounced off boulders, penning Sol and Luna in as they pressed back to back, peering outwards into the enigmatic darkness.

"The wind," Sol repeated. He was shivering. Luna could feel the vibrations in his body, hear them in his voice.

She spun and tugged at his arm as if it were the rope of a bell tower and she was sounding the warning. "Something's out there."

"It could be a person."

A flashing vision crossed Luna's mind. It was the hairy face she'd seen in the mirror—grotesque, horrifying, close.

It's not a person.

A shudder ran down her spine. She desperately wanted to escape, if only from the darkness which closed in around them. It was only its masking black veil which made all of this seem real. She goaded Sol with a jab of her finger. "Get your torch out and have a look."

"That'll draw attention. I don't want it to know where we are."

Luna shuddered with cold certainty.

It knows where we are.

"The light might scare it away," she said, but this was bullshit. The light might banish her fears or it might reveal them—it was a terrible gamble. Life or death stakes, the OCD right for a change.

She hummed the nursery rhyme.

"Stop that," said Sol, flicking on the torch.

The light illuminated the underside of Sol's face like a storyteller reaching the climax of their ghost tale around the campfire. The deep shadows made his features look ape-like, the brows heavy, the eye sockets sunken, and the cheekbones too big. He flashed a smile to reassure her, but it did nothing of the sort. His gums looked blood red in the harsh glare, his teeth yellow and sharp.

Luna took a step away, giving him a shove as if offering him to the darkness.

Take him, not me. I'm going to be a mother.

Sol swung the light around, and he disappeared into nothing more than the silhouette of his outstretched arm, a beam of illumination extending from it like an accusing finger. Luna looked in that direction.

Who, or what, is out there scaring the life out of us?

There was movement in the trees. The swishing branches sounded like a rawhide lash being shaken out, ready to deliver punishment for sins past and present. Dread footfalls pounded like a club over Luna's head, mortal blows to end this suffering. Luna hunched as if in pain, grasping her stomach protectively.

Oh, God. Get me out of this and I'll keep the baby.

She heard a moan and couldn't be sure if it were her or whatever was out there who made it. A rush of displaced air washed over her, the heavy steps picking up their pace. Sol slashed the beam of light protectively before him like a sword. It caught a glimpse of a hulking shape as it swept past, and he snapped the torch back to that spot. A huge silhouette reared out of the darkness. The moan rose to a roar so loud it made the night air shudder. Reality itself seemed to vibrate as terror gripped Luna's heart, arteries and veins in her head squeezing tight, the pressure like a vice around her skull.

Sol screamed as the illuminating beam of his torch met the face of the thing charging through the forest. Ferocious fangs protruded from a gaping mouth which split an ugly ape visage, pink tongue pulsing like an internal organ and spittle flying. Its red eyes were fixated on Sol like burning chunks of coal in sunken pits, framed by dark, hair-covered flesh. It was a vision of hell, a demon of Luna's nightmares made real.

Time slowed, thoughts moving like treacle in sluggish neurons. Luna was frozen, body stiff, lungs paralysed by ice, unable to make a sound. Even the counting of the OCD in her head was silent, finally stifled by a true source of fear, all mental illusion banished by the dread reality of the monster before her.

Here was death manifested—bigfoot.

6

The creature bore down on them like a runaway truck, monstrous bulk and pulsing, powerful muscles rippling under hairy skin. Luna flinched as it missed her by inches, instead choosing Sol as its target. It body slammed into him with a bone crunching impact, the sound reverberating. It was simultaneously like a slab of meat being slapped down and a bundle of sticks being snapped, and was accompanied by the ear-splitting roar of the monster. Blood flecks spattered Luna's face, some entering her open mouth. The hot bitter taste was enough to rouse her from her shocked state.

She found she could do nothing but scream, her limbs gone to jelly. Her cry of terror was lost in the crashing impact of Sol's body breaking tree branches and the passing of the monster. The earth shook beneath its weight.

Then it stopped. Sol flopped to the ground, a limp, lifeless doll, his face a crumbled mask illuminated by his torch. Death had robbed him of personality. He looked like a slaughtered carcass, a great split of ruptured flesh running up his side, through which blood and guts seeped into the dirt. A rain of leaves fluttered down to cover him like a shroud.

The bigfoot turned slowly and deliberately on tree trunk-thick legs, the feet appearing almost human, yet massive in size, stomping up clouds of dust. Luna sobbed as its pitiless red eyes fixed on her with a baleful stare. The bloodshot eyeballs were almost human, but they showed no pity, no compassion, only mad fury. A squirt of hot reeking piss ran down the inside of Luna's thigh.

Sniffing the air, the monster's ugly face scrunched up, with its fat pink tongue peeping obscenely between bulbous lips, tasting the air like a snake. It shook its head in dissatisfaction, stomped down with one foot towards Luna. She whimpered but could not run, aware of the avalanche of muscle which would fall on her if she fled. The bigfoot raised arms stronger than those of the largest bodybuilder, flexing biceps like kegs, huge veins popping through a covering of thick hair. It straddled Sol's corpse and jumped from one foot to the other, a victory dance, ham-sized fist beating its chest as it gloated over its kill, a triumphant shout bellowing from a broad, barrel chest, pumping like a bellows to assault Luna's ears.

She recoiled, pushed back a step by the fury of that sonic blast. It was an involuntary reflex, but that slight movement triggered a primal hunting mechanism in the bigfoot's brain, a honed and perfected instinct sharpened to a fine point over many years and countless encounters. The monster moved faster than Luna thought possible for something so big. Her own fight or flight kicked in with a stab of adrenaline through her body, but by the time she turned to run it had already reached her, sweeping its arm around like a wrecking ball.

The huge fist pulped her head to jelly as it was struck clean off. A jetting spray of arterial blood spurted up from the gaping hole in her neck as she flopped to the ground like a decapitated chicken. There she spasmed and twitched, mere remnants of neurological signals bouncing around an empty husk devoid of a brain. Soon even these movements ended. There would be no more thoughts, no more numbers—the OCD countdown finally complete, the ultimate fear realised. Here was the end for Luna, and for her unborn baby, not even a beginning.

7

Just as the last sparkling fireworks of dying neurons were going off in Luna's body, on the other side of the mountain there were festivities in progress. Here was vibrant life, the mirror of death. This was the flipside of the coin, flashing and spinning in the air as a whimsical universe decided the fate of those who thought themselves masters of their lives.

Fire twirlers spun their staves, weaving intricate patterns of flames like afterimages of a burning sun on the eyes of the revellers. Bongos and djembe drums were played with ever-increasing energy, calloused hands pounding the skins, the drummers in a circle surrounding the twirlers. Strange shouts and bird calls were made by people in colourful costumes as they strutted like peacocks on a lawn, their clothes part hippie, part fairy tale, all weird.

The smell of marijuana was in the air, but this was hardly the only drug being consumed, though it was the most conspicuous and ubiquitous. Others had, discretely or flamboyantly, downed pills and tabs, or ate mushrooms harvested from cow shit in fields during the weeks leading up to the event, heedless of their earthy source, or otherwise believing it brought them closer to Mother Nature.

There were tents set up nearby, though few people had retired to these this early. Those that were occupied shook with frenetic energy, sending out orgiastic vibrations into the shimmering haze of the bonfire burning at the centre of the camp. Sparks and embers drifted into the air, trailing off into the forest like sprites dashing amongst the tree trunks.

Victor frowned at these in disapproval, but said nothing, in this world but not of it. He was a spectator, a visitor—strange as this seemed to him, as these people were in *his* national park.

Above his head, a more benevolent visage watched over them like a departed spirit. The bright face of the moon shone through a hole in the clouds like a spotlight, checking in on this strange display of hedonistic excess and fire hazards just as Victor did also. It seemed to smile, willing to leave well enough alone and be at peace, but as it blinked its crater eyes behind a wisp of clouds, its mouth changed to one of shock, as if witnessing something terrible, happening now, or about to happen, somewhere else in the expansive national park.

Victor grimaced, scratched at the stiff starched collar of his park ranger uniform, and reached down to his hip for a weapon which was absent. The gun in its fake leather holster was a phantom which might never have existed, a figment of his imagination reflecting how he saw himself rather than reality. Even so, he felt naked without it, despite being fully clothed amongst these half-naked savages. He patted his belt where it would have been, not feeling at all reassured. The gun would not only have provided protection—and power—but its metal solidity could have anchored him in a way sorely missed in this dreamy world of frolicking drug takers. Without it, he felt exposed, not sure others would obey him. Even his beloved forest felt like it could turn on him. The trees no longer felt familiar but ominous, no longer his home and hunting ground, but a place where monsters stalked the darkness.

They really should issue us guns. Then I wouldn't have to be afraid of my own shadow.

Still, it wasn't all bad. Perched on a fat log—a tree he'd cut down himself with a chainsaw years ago—he felt like a dignitary from a civilised nation on a diplomatic mission to a savage tribe. They banged their drums, did their primitive dances, and plied him with beverages which he politely refused. The same could not be said for Wright. She took the beers as they were brought to her in an endless procession, though she at least refused the joints and other, more exotic gifts the people offered up to them, laying them on blankets at their feet as if they were gods to be feted.

And in a way, this was true. In this domain their power was godlike and omnipotent. As park rangers, Victor and Wright had the ability to shut this whole thing down—there were more than enough codes being violated to do so. Victor at least still had enough of his head on his shoulders to make that call if he felt like it, though Wright seemed to have completely lost hers, knocked clean off by the drink and the heady atmosphere. The front of her ranger uniform was unbuttoned, the collar loose, revealing more than a little cleavage. And though not matching some of the more scantily clad women at the revel for sheer lasciviousness, to Victor that glimpse was more tantalising and sexy than the faceless waves of undulating flesh which passed him by as the dancers got into the rhythm of the drum circle. In his eyes they were not people as Wright was a person to him, and he stored the sight of her like this away for a lonely night out in a mountain cabin on fire watch.

As ironic as that concept is now, he thought as he watched the fire breathers ready buckets and cups, their unlit torches laid out on blankets, all of it reeking of kerosene.

"Wright, all this is a major fire hazard," he said with a sweep of his hand, loud enough to send the nearest partygoers into fresh, frantic acts of obeisance. They tried in vain for Victor to take anything, and when they realised nothing was working, they turned to Wright and plied her even harder than before in compensation, colourful bottles of exotic liquor floating around her head like fairy lights, tipping occasionally like bowing courtiers to flow their contents into cups.

Wright took a shot, then a second, and undid another button.

"Can you lighten up?" she said, her face a ruddy red in the firelight. "If we tried to keep every person who visited the park up to spec, no one would visit at all."

"That's not true," he replied. "We get plenty of families and hikers, not to mention the scout troops. They're all well behaved."

"They shit on the trails and leave behind rubbish for us to pick up," sneered Wright.

"I don't think these people are any cleaner." He wrinkled his nose up at the stench of essential oils and sweat. Leaning in closer to the bonfire, he inhaled deeply to cleanse his nostrils with the familiar smoky scent.

"See, you like the fire as much as the next person," said Wright with a nod.

"As long as it doesn't get out of hand." Victor watched the sparks drifting on the breeze. The glittering sprites took on a spiteful edge as they disappeared into the undergrowth, planting seeds of future chaos.

"It's contained in the fire pit you dug, isn't it?" said Wright. "We're sitting on the logs you cut yourself. This campsite is by your design. These people are using it for the purpose it was intended."

Victor bit his tongue and kept his thoughts to himself.

This is never what I envisioned. Not for this site, and not for my career in the park service. I wish I could take a chainsaw to all this.

Wright paid him no mind anyway. She accepted another shot glass of liquor, tossed it on the bonfire, an offering of her own to show that nature, and not herself, was the ultimate arbiter in the park. This seemed to carry a lot of weight with the revellers, who repeated her action as if honouring the spirit of the forest in the flames of the fire.

Victor was less impressed by such charlatan showmanship.

We all look up to someone. And for me that is no longer Chief Ranger Wright.

As if to prove this point, Wright continued, "And they've paid their camp fees in full." She patted the chest pocket of her uniform. It bulged with more than her ample breasts.

Victor sucked his teeth and curled his lip.

More than in full, I'm sure.

He felt sick with himself all of a sudden. The liquor might not tempt him, but with park ranger pay being what it was…

With a shake of his head he tried to clear the heady temptation of Wright and the kickbacks.

"We should be getting back, we've got a big day tomorrow," he said to her. The partiers nodded along in agreement like the Jesus bobble head on the dash of his truck.

If this is what they get up to when we're around, I shudder to guess what happens the second our backs are turned. Still, they've paid for their privacy, and I don't need money to want to look away from this mess.

The fire breathers had their torches lit now. They sent flaming plumes up from their kerosene-spitting mouths. Victor stuck out his tongue in disgust.

Who's going to want to kiss them later?

He looked at Wright, the liquor forming a moist reflective sheen on her mouth, catching the firelight in a sparkling display of warning like the back of a fluorescent frog. He let out a long sigh.

Who, indeed?

"Come on, time to go," he said, getting up and brushing the flakes of ash from his uniform. It reminded him of the time he'd spent a whole week fighting a raging bushfire, and he shuddered to think he was kindling that sort of trouble again just for the sake of his boss. He wondered if he should do something to prevent the type of terrible event he felt was looming over them.

And who exactly would I report to? It's just me and her for this whole damned park. It's not like the government has the funding to give more of a shit.

"Make sure you clean up when you're done. I want this place to be spotless," he said to everyone and no one. The nodding heads continued to nod as if they heard and understood, eager to get rid of him with false promises. "And make sure you keep that damned fire contained in the pit," he growled like a bear.

And your sins contained to this campsite.

The gold cross hung around his neck felt hot against his chest, heated by its proximity to the fire, or perhaps to this whole situation. Ignoring it—because if he didn't he would have to face up to worse crimes committed by himself against his immortal soul—he caught Wright under the armpit as she struggled to rise. She stumbled, nearly went over into the fire, but Victor caught her, as he always did, and dragged her back at the last second before she was burned by her own folly.

He shook his head, thought about letting her go, seeing how long it took for her to fall foul of herself without him to save her. The bonfire made him sweat, and for a moment he considered loosening his collar. Instead, he bore the heat stoically and dragged the reluctant Wright away from her place of honour on the log—a drunken Bacchus presiding over a fool's court.

You'll have to content yourself with a warm cot and sleeping it off, my liege. In the morning you can count your money as you nurse your hangover.

As he half-carried her to their truck, Victor's hand brushed against her chest, but whether it was to grasp the temptation of the cash or the flesh beneath, not even he knew. He pulled his hand away as if his fingers had touched a flame he didn't want to admit was nestled in his own breast.

I'm an enabler. I share in this sin.

He nearly dropped Wright—she was too heavy a burden for him to carry. A part of him wanted her to fall in the mud they had churned up earlier turning their truck at the head of the road to the campsite. Then she'd have to wallow in the filth she had created. But Victor knew he had created it too. He looked back at the campsite he had built with his own hands and saw what it had become. The cross around his neck suddenly felt heavy indeed.

I need to do something to change. I just don't know how.

"Let's get you back to the cabin," he said to Wright, propping her against the truck as he opened the door.

That's all I can achieve for now. Hopefully tomorrow there's something more to be done.

Wright tumbled into the truck under her own weight, which was a relief for Victor, who went around to the other side of the cab, and climbed in. As he started the truck, the revellers fired up a laser light show, the colourful beams cutting across each other like a science fiction sword fight.

Looking back in his rear view mirror as he drove down the road, he couldn't help but see this colourful display as a beacon, inviting all sorts of trouble its way.

8

Arlo watched the park ranger's truck trundle down the road out of the campsite. The tail lights of the vehicle left persistent neon glow streams of colour in his vision, setting off further sparklers of chemical pleasure in his brain.

"Alright, yeah, that's awesome," he said to Tarise, licking his lips and nodding. "Now we can really get this party started."

He filled a bucket from a jerry can, the fumes pungent and dizzying. Trying to be careful, yet sloshing plenty on the ground, he threw the fuel on the fire. A huge fireball curled into the overhanging branches of the trees and licked the face of the moon in the sky. Awed *oohs* rose up in unison from the revellers. Tarise danced back from the flames which spread out in tendrils along the trails of spilled fuel with a delighted yet terrified squeal.

I wonder if she realises those butterfly wings she's got on are flammable, thought Arlo. He gave her a maliciously playful shove back towards the bonfire, an experiment to see what would happen. She squealed again, more like a stuck pig this time, and it stabbed something in Arlo's brain which was dark yet alluring, spiking off a cascade of chemically induced fantasies he saw as he looked deep into the flames, the hallucinations alive, bodies writhing in agony and ecstasy simultaneously.

"Don't do that, you idiot," said Harmony, grabbing Tarise's arm to haul her away to a safe distance. Arlo reflexively snapped his own grip on her other arm to claim her, and for a minute Tarise was the rope in a tug of war between them.

"Stop that. You can share, can't you?" said Tarise, giggling in her affected schoolgirl manner. She had gone limp, all her free will abandoned for the moment, though this was her own choice. It was part of their group dynamic, a love triangle where two sides were longer than the third. Arlo pulled a little harder on Tarise's arm, trying to get a bit more than his fair share. He felt her soft skin roughen beneath his hard grasp and wondered if she would let him burn her a bit.

Maybe she'd let me brand her—my initials in a love heart.

If she consented to that, it was unclear what exactly she'd let he and Harmony do to her if they chose, and how far they'd go themselves. Lines began to blur, the borders of consent shifting physically across the landscape of Tarise's body as he and Harmony pulled her first one way and then another. Tarise continued to giggle, satisfied to be the centre of attention.

Seeing beyond Tarise as if she weren't real, Arlo locked eyes with Harmony. Her blue eyes were shards of ice, and fixed him with a hard stare which cooled his passions a touch, or transformed them, sending his mind down another path, his mind flipping from pain to pleasure in an instant as if both were one and the same, just different expressions of the same desire. Harmony mirrored his feelings, and he hallucinated, bringing them into physical manifestation. Her already large nose elongated and took on a woody texture, exposing the lie that she was Tarise's saviour. This made Arlo smile a feral grin.

You want to use her as much as I do.

He felt a part of his own anatomy getting longer and harder, but he knew that was no lie. It poked out from the loin cloth he wore, his only attire. Harmony's cool gaze snapped down on it. The look on her face told Arlo this was an unwelcome development, not because sex was off the table, just premature, that he'd blown his load too early by exposing his hand in this way.

Embarrassed, with the shame amplified by the drugs he was on, he let go of Tarise. She sprung away from him like a released spring and fell into Harmony's arms, swooning with a low moan of pleasure, happy to have something decided for her. Harmony scooped her up like a child, rocking her back and forth with a soft lullaby. Tarise closed her eyes, letting Harmony take her where she would.

Arlo wiped the sweat from his forehead, smearing the body glitter he'd applied there earlier. He stepped back from the heat of the fire, his feathers ruffled, so he rearranged the colourful plumage in his hair. Some of the feathers fell out. They flew skyward in the updraft from the fire, carried like burning embers on the wind, and were lost somewhere in the trees. Arlo felt naked without them, like a balding bird. He tried to regain some dignity, strutting around like a cock, his wattle hanging loose between his legs, flashing with each thrust of his dancing hips.

He was no more absurd than the rest of the partiers, all of them lost in their drugs, or in the spectacle of the lasers carving up the night sky, or otherwise focused on their own lusts and distractions, the fireworks going off in their brains invisible behind glassy eyes, moist and flashing in the glow of the bonfire. Arlo saw his own face mirrored in those eyes, miniature versions of himself staring back, distorted in the curved lenses, reflecting his faults.

He felt pity and shame, the drugs turning on him. Sweat poured down his back like a waterfall, his skin tingling as electric panic spread along frayed nerves. He searched frantically for some relief, saw Harmony and Tarise dancing. They were like a hazy mirage, promising an oasis in a desert. His mouth suddenly felt dry. He was dying for water. Trying to look nonchalant, but instead shambling like a clubfoot hunchback, he sidled up to them, adding a pointy edge to form the triangle which jutted uncomfortably into all their sides.

Harmony growled like a protective mother lion, yet did nothing more to chase him away. Over time she softened through forgetfulness and the long night faded into one long string of cascading moments, each blurring one into another, until the bonfire burned down to coals, its orange glow replaced by the rising sun setting the horizon ablaze.

By then, Arlo, Harmony, and Tarise had fucked, or fought, or danced more—it didn't matter, because they couldn't remember much, those moments lived but then lost in the drifting haze of hedonistic abandon.

Besides, to these three they were pretty much the same thing anyway, one blurring into the other until all sense of individuality was lost and all actions flowed like a river from one point to another, seamlessly and headless of direction or purpose.

This was the life they had chosen, or which had chosen them. Either way, they were locked in to it, addicted to far more than the drugs.

***

I can't let go, thought Arlo, fiddling with a pouch in his tent. Harmony and Tarise were sleeping next to him. He had not slept at all. He'd not had the blissful release of unconsciousness, with its clear cut line between intoxication and the waking to sobriety, only to then get fucked up again after being well rested. Instead he felt like he had slowly faded, the colour draining from life until all he saw was a grey haze of smoke—not pleasant and welcoming, like that of weed, but suffocating, as if he were in a house on fire and sought only to escape. His consciousness was stretched thin, his mind a tightrope he could no longer balance upon. He constantly felt like he was falling over, his sight tumbling downwards like water cascading off a cliff.

With trembling fingers, he pulled the drugs out of the pouch. The tabs would take too long for them to kick in—the relief from the cold dawn of reality could not wait. Instead he chose the powder, desperate to banish his depression in a quick rush.

His head pounded, or maybe that was just the music, electronic dance beats rattling the poles of the tent, pumping the tent's sides like the membrane of a heart. His own heart beat harder as he snorted the line of artificial happiness. With it, he found he could finally stand. He had to bow like a slave in the close confines of the tent, and this irked him, because he felt powerful. He shook Harmony and Tarise, sleeping in a naked, tangled heap at his feet. They groaned and shifted like a grotesque, two headed, eight limbed monster. He sprung back from them in fright, decided to leave them be, lest his own flesh meld into that horrifying amalgam. He burst forth from the tent like a butterfly from its cocoon, ready for a new day, a new life, where the past was forgotten with all its ugly and constricting forms. He spread his wings and flew as the music took a hold of him.

9

Victor cupped his hands around a steaming mug, trying to wake up and annoyed he'd slept in so late. He was staring at a map of the national park as if surveying his kingdom. Even though it was a paper map push-pinned to the wall of the cabin, to him it was a dynamic, three-dimensional thing full of details gained through long association and experience. Memories played like a movie in his imagination as he took in each location his eyes darted across, and these sparked off thoughts of future possibilities, extrapolations and extensions of the past. Half of a ranger's job was to predict trouble, to put together pieces which pointed to some looming catastrophe—changes in the weather, reports of wild animals, rock falls, broken bridges, and many other things besides. There were a lot of angles to cover from this small cabin with nothing but a radio, a satellite phone, and an aging laptop with bad internet coverage.

This map was the simplest of his tools, yet the one he relied on the most. It was a version of the park now dated, a colour aerial photo with contour lines and grids overlaid in yellow and white. This single snapshot of the whole park made the expanse of forests and mountains look sterile, locked in time and place, a finished masterpiece with all the information set in stone. But really the park was a dynamic force of nature, ready to humble man at every opportunity. He knew as well as any that while it was a place of serenity and peace, it could turn deadly in a moment. He'd had to haul more than one corpse off the mountain range with his own hands in his time, and that never got any easier, no matter how many times he'd done it. If he could prevent such a disaster by his vigilance, he would, and his gut was telling him to be on alert, even as the birds sang peacefully in the trees outside and the sun shone through the window, casting a warm glow on his little world inside the cabin.

Blowing on his coffee, he squinted through the rising steam, trying to piece together clues which weren't forthcoming. He had little to go on, basically just a hunch, but something was irking him, a sixth sense itching at the back of his head like a spider's bite. He knew every square kilometre— or mile, the scale on the side of the map conveniently had both—of the park, all its nooks and crannies, its abundant wonders, as well as its hidden secrets. He knew it was trying to speak to him now.

He took a long gulp from his mug, trying to swallow something black and foul—a truth he couldn't face. But whether it was about him or the park he couldn't yet tell, though he suspected its source. There was snoring from the bed behind him, and the loud rasping breathing was like that of a wild beast hibernating. Doing his best to ignore it, he peered at the map more intently, willing it to give up its secrets.

In the middle of the map was a word in bold—Nightcap. It reminded him of something and Victor lifted a hand to his head, wincing.

Why did I let Wright talk me into a drink before bed?

She grunted and coughed in her sleep, and started snoring again. He turned to look at her, seeing in that bed a mirror of his own sin, her naked breasts pointing accusing nipples at him like the stiff fingers of the dead, punishing his lack of vigilance with guilt. He scratched at his crotch unconsciously, a lingering tingle of pleasure there, numbed by the passage of time, now a bad memory of regret. This was a mistake he thought he wouldn't repeat after the last time.

Yes, but I get so lonely, and I'm only human.

He shook his head, denying the validity of any rationalising. He did not want to feel human, as it tore him away from his true calling. The chain around his neck felt heavy, the cross a burden he couldn't bear. He took his coffee out onto the balcony. Here the park took on its living, breathing quality, the air rich with its aromas, rising up from the valley below, the trees spread out like a blanket, then parting to make way for the mountain ranges bursting up through them like colossal rocks thrust up through the ground like an earthquake.

He was relieved to see no broad swathes of fire having consumed the forest in the night, and perhaps Wright's laxity on the ravers could be excused. It helped ease the guilt he felt about his own cut of the money padding his hip pocket.

No harm, no foul.

He smiled, but that spider was still biting the back of his head, goading him to action. He couldn't rest easy, not like Wright, who had been made irresponsible by the long years of independent action out here in the park, where the ranger was the only law. Victor wasn't that jaded, not yet, but it was a slippery slope, all too easy to slide down. There were those willing to pay for them to turn a blind eye, whether it was hunters wanting to hunt out of season, or people dumping rubbish, or campers caught without a permit, or whatever it was, and it was easy to justify. After all, there were worse things.

He scratched the itch on the back of his head. It wasn't going away, but he decided he could ignore it, downing the rest of his hot coffee, burning his mouth but ignoring that too. He went back inside, stood over Wright, who was still snoring, head thrown back and mouth open. Victor made a face. It wasn't her best look.

He resisted the urge to wake her up. Instead, he climbed back into bed and stared at her naked breasts, trying to unlock the memories of pleasure drink had blurred. They seemed as hazy as they had the night before, obscuring his best judgement and leading him astray.

***

Arlo danced all day and into the early evening, carried on a wave of euphoria, fatigue masked by the drugs. The DJ was his god, jerking his limbs like a puppet master, and he found that he could not stop—not that he wanted to, addicted to the dance and its cascade of good feelings. In time, Harmony and Tarise joined him, and the three of them formed their imitation of a perfect triangle, each bouncing off each other at equal angles for the time being, so that each got the attention they needed, passing it on in turn. All was in balance, their love delusional yet seemingly real for them, demonstrating the ideal of what their relationship could be. Though mostly artificially sustained by the substances they had ingested, it was continued by their commitment to this life, and each other, none of them wanting to come back down and touch the bald face of reality.

Later, when the drugs or their bodies ebbed low, things would take a turn for the worse, but for now, they were in sync, the forces of nature flowing through their bodies even as nature planned to betray them. A great game was being played out on a level they did not understand, a single, powerful piece on the move, ready to smash their unity and happiness. Arlo had little hint of this, other than the rough edge of the drugs with the usual chances of them turning on a person. He shook the feeling off, blinking to clear the hallucination of faces forming in the trees.

They were ugly, and he hated everything ugly. He looked at Harmony and Tarise, saw nothing but beauty in them, the same beauty he saw in all the dancers around them, a mass of perfect humanity, totally delusional, pretending they held no judgements even as they were secretly the harshest critics of each other.

And even more so of themselves, though it was lucky there were no mirrors out here in the bush, only projections—of the perfect self, perfect relationships, and perfect feelings. The dancers formed and dissolved their configurations, their interactions manifesting as invisible shapes which spun in the air. Into these fragile prisms of glass they sent forth love and light which bounced through angles no longer perfect, but flawed, no one person getting the love they needed as they fought with each other for scraps. All the while they pretended like nothing of the sort was happening—on a shallow level they remained deeply committed to an ideal where all was bright and happy. Hidden beneath—just skin deep—was an undercurrent of infidelity and betrayal.

The music was pure though—that at least did not betray. It held Arlo aloft by strings which tugged him this way and that, made sure he didn't have to make any decisions, all his movements beyond his control, with no responsibility taken or required. Anything he did was out of his hands, the drugs in charge, creating a bubble of safety and escape. But beyond this ephemeral barrier a breeze howled through the trees, sounding like a wild beast come to claim an ancient tithe.

A shiver ran through the crowd in response, at first ignored and then quickly forgotten. It became the shimmy of a dance move, the drugs rattling through veins, stirring the nervous systems of the revellers and pumping blood which flowed hot like fever dream thoughts.

Flesh—that's all Arlo saw, all any creature born of this world would see in what surrounded him. For him it stirred lust and a desire for control, precisely because he had no control over his own life, and he knew it. Only in sex, drugs, and dance could he reclaim all that—through another person, if that's what it took.

But there was something else watching him, watching them all, and it was not sex it saw in the flesh, but living meat, ripe for the plucking. Intelligent, reddened eyes blinked from beneath a fallen tree, a blanket of moss draped over hulking shoulders as camouflage. The creature did not move, despite its vast bulk. A bird landed on its back, pecking at hairy skin exposed through patches in the moss, seeking lice and ticks. Stirring with a low, threatening rumble, the moss flexed like the ground above an active geyser, ready to explode into an eruption of violent force at any moment. The bird shifted its footing uneasily, its head bobbing back and forth. The surface beneath its splayed feet settled and so did the bird. It went back to pecking its sharp beat into a crevice of skin, rummaging around like a knife.

The bigfoot huffed out a sharp breath of quelled frustration like the hoot of a predatory owl. The bird's wings snapped open and it took off in fright. None of the dancers saw or heard this, noted any change in the regular ebbs and flows of the forest. For all their self-identification as nature lovers, they knew nothing of its ways.

Unlike the bigfoot, who had waited a long time and could wait a short time more. The long winter of its hibernation was over—measured in many years. Now the season of the hunt had come.

And here before it was its prey, oblivious to the presence of the monster, enjoying the last day of their lives in wild abandon, as if on some subconscious level they knew and were determined to gain some small measure of pleasure from this, their final dance.

10

Victor gained no small pleasure in being organised, and he sat down at the computer in the cabin to write up his reports and check the logs. He felt a gnawing guilt in his guts, but that could be the soured alcohol fermenting there, turned rancid from mingling with too much strong black coffee. He'd spent about as long as he'd dared watching Wright sleep, as he feared her waking to find him ogling her. Then she'd remember what they'd done and regret it, and it would never happen again. Victor stabbed at the delete key on his keyboard to erase the bad wording of the line he had written.

I don't want it to happen again myself.

Like the poachers they were constantly doing battle with, Victor was forced to cover he and Wright's tracks, falsifying their report about the rave—or did they call it a bush doof here?—so that it looked like they'd shut it down. He was really hanging their arses out on a ledge, because if anything went wrong…

Nothing's going to go wrong. They're just some kids dancing around a fire pit. But who knows what might happen with drugs involved?

Victor cursed, aware he was going to have to go and check on them again. And that would look nothing like doing his duty and everything like sniffing around for another bribe.

Of course, if they want to give me more, I won't say no.

He shook his head, angry with himself. It made the cross around his neck jingle.

"Oh, God, is there any coffee?" groaned Wright, sitting up in the bed. Her fat tits swung like a sow's udders, looking a deep red-pink from greedy piglets sucking on them all night. Victor flushed a similar shade and tried not to look too guilty as he stabbed at the keyboard with his forefingers.

"Yeah, there's some on the stove," he said, keeping his back to her, making it seem like he was respecting her privacy somewhat. Not that she was modest. He heard her scratching at her pubic hair like someone undoing Velcro. Out of the corner of his eye he saw a blurred shadow of movement, a silhouette which conjured up a haunting memory. He twisted his head slightly, caught a glimpse of her pale skin, and he jumped in his seat as if he'd seen a ghost. Wright did moan like a tortured poltergeist, her hangover rattling her bones, giving her the shakes from the withdrawals.

Victor resolved not to look again, pretending it was Medusa herself who assailed him, seeking to turn him to stone. He heard the hissing of her snake hair, but realised it was the sound of the coffee being poured. She slurped at it noisily, a monster gulping down blood. He felt drained by her, his soul empty, needing to be refilled with something, anything, to replace what had been taken.

"I need to Irish up this coffee," she said, leaning over his shoulder to grasp a bottle on the desk. He caught a whiff of her demonic breath, sulphurous as the deepest levels of hell, and found that it was he who regretted what they did last night.

And I definitely don't want it to happen again, he told himself, keeping his eyes on his work.

***

The bigfoot stirred in the underbrush, remembering the night before—the blood, the slaughter—and became impatient for the killing to begin now the sun had dipped low, the moon sprung up in its place like a pale impostor.

Out of the corner of his eye, Arlo saw movement, and the first spikes of fear tainted his euphoria. But it wasn't the monster he saw. Instead, it was something else he dreaded much more. Harmony was dragging Tarise away into the forest. They were giggling and stopping to kiss occasionally, devouring each other hungrily. Arlo snarled like a beast, the drugs beading into balls of sweat on the open pores of his skin. He shook them off, just as he shook off his surroundings, the rave fading into a kaleidoscopic tunnel not of colour, but of grey-scale. The shifting and tumbling shapes he saw were nothing but fragments of his shattered heart, the jagged edges slicing his eyeballs and making him bleed tears of colourless blood.

He took a trembling step forward. Harmony and Tarise tensed, rearing up like alert prairie dogs, heads on a swivel. He froze, but they saw him looking at them. They scattered like startled birds, flying off into the trees with flapping wings strapped to their backs. The beautiful butterfly patterns traced on them in glitter were a red smear which trailed after them, hanging in the air like a blood scent.

Red—the colour had entered Arlo's grey sight. It trickled down across his vision like slow moving molasses. He could smell it, bitter and tangy, and, as it reached his mouth, it was hot iron in the forge, a weapon he would use to get what he wanted, what had been denied to him by this betrayal.

They're going off without me. They don't want me. They don't need me.

His breathing was ragged and laboured, his body exhausted from the dance, the drugs no longer buoying him up artificially. Now they only warped his perception, and he had to stumble forward like the dehydrated zombie he was, with only thin stick legs to prop him up like walking canes. He reached into the leather pouch hanging on a thin strap around his shoulders, desperate for anything to bring him back.

There was no ecstasy left—the girls had taken all his joy. There was a sheet of acid, and he pulled it out, stared at it like a note which told him of rejection, a girl long ago in primary school having written to politely rebuff his advances, sounding all the more cruel in her cold logic as she listed why they weren't suited for each other. Wanting to be rid of the gross memory, and what it meant for him now, he rammed the sheet of acid into his mouth, consumed it hungrily with bestial growls and gnashing teeth.

Then, finding it did nothing to satisfy him or his hunger, he stumbled towards the trees and the darkness which waited there.

***

"It's dark out," said Victor, getting up to stretch after hours of paperwork on the computer. Wright was back on the bed. She'd managed to put on her uniform, but that seemed to be all the work she had planned for the day. A wet towel was draped over her eyes. She was hiding from the world, the world hidden from her.

Unfortunately Victor could still see, still remember he had certain responsibilities.

"Those hikers, the young couple, they're overdue," he said. He went over to the map, traced a line, his finger following a trail he knew the couple were taking.

One, two, three, he counted the distances in his head, the number of days it would take them to walk their route, and realised, yes, they were overdue. That wasn't good.

"Of course, they might be taking their merry old time, lingering by a waterfall or something," he said with a smile, which quickly turned to a frown of worry as he considered other possibilities. He'd seen disaster unfold like this before, seemingly so benign. He slapped his fist into a palm. "If only they'd let us put trackers on their ears."

He went back to the computer, opened up a window to look at the national park in another way. There were hundreds of coloured dots moving jerkily across a simplified black and white line map of the park, overlaid with a red grid. These were the animals they had tagged. The dots were a riot of chaotic movement, like a dance he didn't know the steps to, or perhaps they were guided by a mathematical equation too complex to understand through observation. They clustered here, spread out there. In one place they seemed to radiate from a single point, as if fleeing something terrifying.

What are you trying to tell me?

He tried toggling the time bar in the bottom right corner, travelling back over days and weeks, watching the patterns of coloured points shift about. It was not an exact science when done like this, not without analysing months of data, checking bird migration habits, the comings and goings at the watering holes, and being aware of the various family units of the bigger mammals—these and so much more went into obtaining any useable analysis and predictions. But even without this he could get a sense of the mood of the national park as a whole, augur something from it. He was a primal soothsayer staring into the steaming guts of an animal sacrificed in exchange for foreknowledge of a looming catastrophe.

That spider was biting the back of his head again. He scratched there with nails he'd been meaning to trim, and then chewed on these nervously in a subconscious plan to avoid this mundane task.

"Can you stop sucking on your fingers like an overgrown baby and get out of here already?" said Wright, not taking the towel from her eyes but writhing around with limbs akimbo like a petulant child.

Ironic that she calls me a baby, thought Victor, but he got up, packing a small backpack with some water, food, emergency blanket, poncho, torch, spare batteries, and other essential supplies—enough to keep him alive but light enough so he could move fast, catch up with the hikers. He'd head in from their end point and hopefully catch them coming out sooner rather than later.

"I don't suppose you're coming with me?" he asked Wright.

She groaned. "I'm sick."

I'm sick of you, thought Victor.

"Someone has to stay here and man the radio," he said, offering her an easy way out. "Oh, that reminds me." He picked up the handheld radio, set it to a channel. He wrote the channel frequency on a Post-it note, stuck it to the screen of the computer. "You see this note?" He pointed at the screen.

"Yes," she said without taking the towel from her eyes.

"Stay in touch," he said, not really expecting her to. "There's also the contact number for those ravers here, maybe call them in the morning, see if everything is okay?"

But Wright was already snoring again, which was the only indication she was still alive. Her face had gone even paler, with a green tinge like a corpse, and her limbs were rigor mortis stiff, held at uncomfortable looking angles. The flesh beneath her uniform was bloated like a balloon, buttons strained and popping. She looked like an overstuffed scarecrow ill-treated by months out in high winds and coming apart at the seams.

Victor shook his head, placed his cap upon it, and tucked his cross back into his shirt as he eased the cabin door closed behind him far too gently, wishing he could give it a good slam and rouse Wright from her slumber of negligence.

But if she got it together how would I look in comparison?

The paper money felt heavy in his pocket, his mouth dry from the drink he'd taken the night before. In penitence, or out of a misplaced sense of duty, he hiked off alone into the forest. An owl on a branch hooted, watching with eyes that penetrated the gloom surrounding Victor like a dark cloud. He scampered up the trail like a fleeing mouse without looking back.

11

"Where are you?" shouted Arlo, or thought it, his mind a loud echo chamber, a fractured house of mirrors, reflecting sound and images back to him in distorted patterns which made no sense. Around him the trees loomed menacingly like executioners draped in black capes, silhouetted against the pale glow of the moonlight. The shapes refracted through the broken prism of his senses to form nightmare impressions— branches lifting axes for the kill, hacking him down, his body used like wood to make some type of structure. He saw a bird's nest in a tree, empty save for cracked open eggs, the chicks having left or been devoured. He felt lonely and abandoned, ready to lie down and die, his body decaying to become part of the forest floor with the decomposing leaves, hoping to one day grow into something strong, but for now soft and dissolute. His degeneracy made him bestial, and he fled from himself, even as his quarry also moved away from him.

He saw glimpses of Harmony and Tarise between the trees, the dark trunks like prison bars, keeping him from them. The pair seemed to be enjoying their freedom on the far side of the jail cell he had made for himself, laughing in pleasure, mocking him, glad to see him suffer, happy to exclude him if it caused him pain.

Running towards these imagined or real shapes of people he loved—or at least desperately wanted to possess—he knew he was the one torturing himself through his desire. The branches of the trees lashed him like whips as he ran the gauntlet of his own discontent, arms outstretched, fingers reaching, focused on trying to touch the gossamer wings of the girls as they flew from him on sparkling trails of moonbeams. The same shafts of light burned him like searing hot irons, making reality too bright. They were the swords of ghosts slashing at him, blinding him with their brilliance as they carved him up.

There was pain, but also numbness, time tumbling away, no moment truly captured, life a cascade of memories being remembered rather than experienced. He looked over his shoulder at his past self as if he was already dead and gone. To the distorted lenses of his eyes his spectral ghost body was merely haunting his last steps, repeating them over and over as he stumbled in circles through the forest, with only the tinkling laughter of the girls to guide him towards a heavenly afterlife, a release from suffering promised but not delivered.

But this wasn't paradise. It was hell, with demons lurking in the form of beautiful women he knew he could not trust. They were sirens, leading him to his doom. Their voices sounded like a stream tumbling over rocks, a babbling brook which told him he wasn't good enough to have either of them, let alone both, and that they would be happier without him.

They wanted to kill him. He knew that now. Then they would be free to love one another in peace. He could be written out of the contract they had made with their lust-filled bodies and hole-punched hearts. But he was their partner, and without him the triangle was distorted and unstable. The pyramid lay on shifting sands, ready to tumble as he, the keystone at the corner, was removed.

The wind howled through the trees like a pleasure moan mixed with grief at what was soon to be lost. His drug-addled mind twisted it into an auditory hallucination, his paranoia acting like a funnel, driving the sound in deep to whistle around the primordial reptile base of his brain. He heard whispered counsel from demonic consciences on both his shoulders, advice spat into his ears like poison. It was tearing him apart like wild horses as they tugged in two directions—the acid he had ingested was etching new words into the contract he'd made with the girls, an addendum which said that if he couldn't have them, no one could.

Arlo chased after the girls, his actions justified by this fresh cosmic law only he bore witness to. He became a monster which sought to possess their bodies, living or dead. But he wasn't the only one—there was another creature which stalked these woods, its instincts driving it towards the same goal.

Nearby, a hulking shape shook off its covering of moss and stalked forward, guided by light and sound to the scene of a future slaughter.

***

There was nothing to guide Victor. No light, no sound. He was alone in the depths of the forest, walking the trail by memory, the moon blotted out by the dense trees which closed in over him like a cocoon. He felt the transformation of his soul take place as he wheedled his way through this tube of foliage, aware he would not be the same when he emerged at the other end.

That's if there is an end to this, he thought.

Not for the first time, he felt like he had lived this moment before. Sometimes it got like that out in the dense woods of the park, with the trees and the tracks all looking the same, like the background of a cartoon repeating over and over endlessly, the days and nights resembling each other so perfectly it felt like time itself ceased to exist and he lived in a single continuous moment.

But surely death is the termination point, where the trail finally ceases. Or would it simply be the beginning of a new one?

It seemed he was walking in circles, though he wasn't lost. The feeling of déjà vu stemmed from the fact he had passed this exact spot countless times on past hikes. He knew the trail so intimately it mattered not if it were night or day. It still felt the same, its contours undulating under his boots like the braille read by a blind man.

And then there was the smell. It was one he was familiar with. Carrying human corpses out of the woods was part of his job. Heart attacks, falls from cliffs, snake bites—there were many dangers, accidental and otherwise. He knew the carnal stink of death in all its many forms and in all stages of putrefaction and decay. The smell was ripe and earthy, like rotting meat with fruity undertones. It was a natural thing, and yet it struck his nostrils like a warning, artificially imposed on his senses. That sharp stench could not be mistaken. It lit up his brain with colour, flashing red. He blinked, trying to clear it, wanting to see reality, not imagination. And he was imagining something terrible despite the familiarity of his surroundings.

A looming presence pressed in from the surrounding darkness. He dared not turn on his torch to dispel his fears—the light would draw attention. But he did wonder whether whatever was out here needed it to see him, as plenty of wild animals had night vision.

Surely it can smell me too.

He felt the breeze caress his skin like the cold hand of death, snatching away the sweet corpse stench and carrying his own fear-sweat smell to the hunter's nose, somewhere downwind.

***

Arlo could smell them. He closed in on that ripe and heady lust scent like a glutton to a feast. He found the girls in a clearing. They were a porcelain statue in living motion, their pale naked skin alabaster white in the moonlight, sparkling with moisture. Locked in coitus, they had merged into a single creature. He was on the outside, separate, looking in on this intimate moment with envy and hate as they stared at each other with love and desire.

"What the fuck do you think you're doing?" he said to them, or himself, he wasn't sure. He heard the words in two voices—one external and loud, the other internal and quiet. Both were judgemental and a shock to the system.

The girls sprung apart like a shattered vase striking the floor. Arlo's heart broke in a similar fashion. He rushed forward, not content with the damage he had already wrought, seeking to further smash the remaining pieces.

Tarise was too quick. She writhed away, her body that of a lithe snake, flowing like water through Arlo's fingers. Harmony didn't try to run. She moved to impose herself between the other two. Arlo ploughed into her and they went over in a tangle of limbs, resembling the statue from before in form if not intent. Hate prevailed over lust even as these two emotions blended into one for Arlo, manifesting as a single action. He wrapped his hands around something thin and fragile, and squeezed. A vein stood out on his forehead as he held firm. There was a series of fragile clicks—the popping of vertebrae, the collapse of a windpipe.

Tarise screamed. Arlo grunted. And Harmony made no more sounds ever again.

12

Victor reached for the Maglite torch at his hip as if reaching for a sidearm. Gone was his surety of the space around him, his familiarity with the woods. Things had changed and he needed to shed light on the situation. Like a bat using sonar, he was deeply aware on an instinctual level that his surroundings were not what he expected—something had happened here, a force unleashed which had altered the landscape.

His nose had led him here to this spot, now it was betraying him, the smells all around, and he knew he was in the epicentre of whatever blood-drenched catastrophe had unfolded in the depths of the national park. His nostrils drew in the bitter iron tang, the caustic stench dripping down the back of his throat. He hawked and spat, then regretted the noise he'd made— silence seemed his only protection available, and even his breathing sounded too loud as he sought to push the sweet smell of death out of his mouth with each exhale.

The torch was in his hand, heavy like the handle of a sword. He hesitated for a moment, not sure he wanted to give away his location. But surely whatever was out there could smell him— and if not him, then the reek of gore wafting in the air would draw attention like a beacon. This site would soon be swarming with scavengers if not predators—though the fact it wasn't already gave him pause. What had scared them away?

He desperately wished he held a gun instead of a torch. There was bear spray in his pack, though that didn't feel like enough. What if there was some type of deranged serial killer out in the woods? He swallowed hard, wrinkled his nose as his guts curdled with the foul taste in the air.

One final deep breath to steel his courage before the plunge—he thumbed the on switch of the torch and the beam of light extended like a long blade to slice the darkness. It didn't illuminate the whole area at once, and he had to sweep it back and forth before him like a defensive parry, seeking to ward off the terrible thing which he was sure was still lurking in the dark.

He caught flashes of red as he played the light around, but he'd been expecting that. Blood was everywhere, an overwhelming scene of carnage to shock the nerves. What he wasn't expecting was the sheer destruction. Trees were snapped off at the base, their trunks thrown about like twigs. Others looked like they had violently exploded. Splinters of wood crunched underfoot as Victor took tentative steps through what had once been dense forest, now a clearing made by the passage of what could only have been the sweep of a heavy wrecking ball. Everything was flecked with blood like a crime scene, the spatters of red a macabre piece of abstract art—one it was impossible for Victor to interpret.

What the hell happened here?

He froze as he heard a creaking sound, and he was unable to turn the torch beam on the source, afraid of what it might reveal. There was silence for a long time, broken by the crackle of the radio coming to life on his belt. Victor jumped out of his skin, reached for it with agitated fingers, turned down the volume after much fumbling and cursing.

Silence prevailed for a while, then the eerie creaking once more.

What's out there?

The hairs on the back of his neck bristled. He took a step backwards, and then another. He bumped into something with his foot, which made him stop. He shone the torch down at the object, but couldn't believe what he was seeing. His sight slid off it like the single tear which cascaded down his cheek—his subconscious knew even as his forebrain denied it.

He swung the torch beam back up as the creaking made him jump again. A branch hung by a thread, scraping against a trunk as it rocked back and forth in a silent breeze. It gave way under its weight, crashing to the ground and breaking in half across a rock. Victor snapped simultaneously and turned to run, his mind clouding with fear, no longer thinking clearly. He tripped on the object from before, fell sprawling in the dirt and leaves beside it. He pointed the trembling finger of the torch beam at the thing. This time he truly saw it for what it was—a severed human leg, red and raw like a butchered hunk of meat.

His scream reverberated through the trees, waking sleeping birds which took flight and scattered, their silhouettes crossing the luminous disk of the moon high above the trees. Their cawing cries were like a call for help no one would answer.

***

The moon's shining face looked down on another terrible scene on the far side of the mountain. Arlo panted hard as he rose and stood over Harmony's dead body, looking down at her glassy eyes. The reflective orbs sparkled in the light like children's marbles. His mind toyed with them, believing she was still alive, watching him, judging him.

The spell was only broken as Tarise screamed again.

Reality snapped as instinct kicked in and took charge. Arlo turned at the same time she did, synchronised like dancers in a way only hunter and prey can be. He galloped after her, but she was swift as a gazelle and outpaced him, goaded by mortal terror.

Arlo felt fear as well, though his own was of something else entirely—retribution, punishment. Tarise would have to be dealt with, one more murder to hide the first. Even his drug fuelled mind knew he had committed some terrible sin he needed to conceal. The only way was more death, and he morphed into his role as executioner seamlessly, the acid providing the means to hallucinate the role-play.

To him it was a sexy, thrilling game.

To Tarise it was life and death.

Their footfalls slapped the ground as they ran through the forest, echoed by others not so far away, the tread of something much bigger. Tarise's screams were similarly repeated by other throats, the terrified sounds of the ravers like that of cornered animals as a predator burst upon them from the treeline.

13

Tarise didn't stop when she reached the clearing where the rave was taking place. She continued, believing she was fleeing to safety. Really she was diving straight into the fire.

Arlo went to follow her in, still trying to run her down and silence her before she gave him away. But something gave him pause, some primal instinct which warned of a violent hierarchy, the rule of the jungle. He wasn't the only predator here. Something much more powerful was hunting, and it claimed precedence. Arlo was the jackal to its lion, a snivelling thing which would have to wait for scraps while the true king prowled for prey. As if pulled up on a leash, he halted and retreated behind some bushes, watched Tarise waving her hands around, frantically trying to attract attention.

She got it.

A large humanoid shape waved its arms about as if mocking her, or perhaps to draw her to it. For a moment, Arlo thought his depth perception was shot by the hallucinatory effects of the acid. To him, it looked like the thing was close, but it was actually beyond Tarise, and thus was a massive creature, much bigger than any man. It stood before the bonfire, a dark outline with long outstretched arms, as if welcoming Tarise into an embrace which promised safety and love.

Instead, the arms enfolded her and she disappeared into the dark mass as if it were a giant black hole which swallowed her. She emerged on the other side of it a crumpled up mass, her limbs folded backwards, her head snapped off. Huge hands emerged from the creature's silhouette, placing her almost gently on the ground by the fire, as if she were a neatly folded bundle to take on a picnic. There were several other such piles there, and Arlo nearly vomited as he realised they were people, his friends and fellow ravers, now reduced to packages of slaughtered meat.

The thing which killed them turned, and, with blinding speed, gave chase after more scattered dancers, who ran around in panic like chickens with their heads cut off. Soon, their decapitated bodies joined the growing pile, their blood leaking onto the grass in glossy smears which caught the light of the bonfire.

Arlo didn't dare move, and he let out a breath only after a long time holding it, only made aware of the fact by the searing pain in his lungs. His exhalation was a low whistle, barely audible, yet the monster in the camp swung its head to look in his direction. Arlo saw the creature more clearly now. The terrible face was that of a huge ape, intelligent and expressive as a man's, yet grotesquely distorted. It sniffed the air with fat nostrils and peeled back fat lips, baring huge yellow fangs. Its humongous hands hung from long arms, gangly yet powerful. The fat sausage fingers clenched and unclenched as if they were already squeezing the life from Arlo's body.

Against all reason, Arlo forced himself not to run. One look at the powerful legs of the monster, with its tree trunk thighs and sinewy calves, was enough to convince him he would be overtaken in seconds. It would snatch him up or otherwise crush him under its massive weight. With the effortlessness of a child doing origami, his body would be creased and folded, put with the rest of the grotesquely broken bodies by the fire.

So, instead of fleeing, he held himself as still as possible, breathed silently. He blinked, trying to clear the terrifying vision before him as if he had conjured it up. He was beginning to think it possible this was all a hallucination.

It's just a bad trip, he told himself.

But it wasn't a bad trip. This was happening. What's more, he knew it to be so. Otherwise he'd get up, step forward, and ask for help. He could do no such thing, his sense of his own mortality a chain around his body, holding him back, locking him in place. He couldn't help but wish things were different though, and his mind played tricks on him, driven by a desire for escape. It was still projecting scenarios of an idyllic world now gone, a world erased by this creature which erased life.

Arlo saw himself dancing, drinking, and singing with his friends. If Tarise accused him of murder, he'd deny it, or claim he was unable to hear the words over the loud music. Her claim that Arlo had killed Harmony—that he'd tried to kill her, too— would be ignored by the others, drowned out by the cacophony of their revelry. They only wanted love and light, not death and darkness, so they would look away.

But death and darkness was what they got anyway. The monster had seen to that. The only light which remained was that of the bonfire. By its glow, Arlo watched the creature scoop up its many parcels of meat like so many Christmas presents in its huge arms, and with them clutched against its chest, carried them away.

It was a long time before Arlo could no longer hear the heavy thuds of its hulking steps, and even longer before he ceased to hear the louder beats of his terror-stoked heart.

14

"Wright, are you there?" Victor said into the radio, unwilling to raise his voice above a terse whisper. The handset crackled and hissed in reply, the sound alien and inhuman, bringing him no comfort. It was also far too loud. He fiddled with the knobs, turning down the static, but in the process he accidentally changed the frequency. This was bad, as he now forgot which channel he had written on that Post-it note, and he clicked back through the frequencies blindly, hearing nothing but more static. He was lost, not in the physical landscape, but in the ether, that invisible place where his fear warbled like the keening cry of a ghost upon the night air. This call was replied by the banshee howl of the wind through the trees, mocking his fear and amplifying it tenfold. Branches shook menacingly like the outstretched arms of monsters, threatening to grab him and crush the life from his body.

They're all around me, closing in.

His own limbs shook. He was a stiff manikin moved by forces beyond his understanding, the dread hand of dark gods closing around his heart. The pain in his chest was a vice closing, and his jaw clamped tight in sympathy as he struggled to cope with it. He tasted the bitter iron tang of blood and realised he was biting his lip, but could not release the rigor mortis lockjaw. Instead he ground his own flesh to a bloody pulp between bony millstones as his head spun around and around.

He heard the voices of demons speak to him in the static of the radio, and his lungs froze in fear so that he couldn't breathe. Not that he could bring himself to risk a breath, wanting no sound to interfere as he strained to hear, transfixed by the possessed device in his hand.

"Victor," it said.

Holy fuck, it knows my name.

"I know you're there," it said. The voice sounded like the icy breeze of a mountainside. It was the exhalation of a monstrous yeti, breathing down his neck. It was not hot and moist like that of the living, but cold and distant, an echo bouncing off a slope of snow.

It triggered an avalanche in Victor's soul. He was up and running, but not before he picked up the only weapon he had to hand. It was stout and hard, a lump of wood perhaps. He didn't care what it was, only that it felt reassuring to swing the thing about. It whooshed through the air satisfyingly, its weight reassuring. It was an awkward thing though, and heavy, but he wasn't letting it slow him down. Adrenaline pumped through his veins, working his legs like pistons, his arms those of a robot in a factory, jerking back and forth, clearing everything before him as he swung his weapon about.

Branches lashed his face but he didn't notice, tiny cuts bleeding into eyes already blinded by the darkness. He'd left his torch behind. A glance over his shoulder—it was back there, shining in the dark like a glowing spectre. But he wasn't going back to get it. That light marked the place of slaughter. It was the warning beacon of a lighthouse, spinning in his terror-mad mind. He paused to shake his weapon back towards the site as if the thing in his hand were a voodoo totem pole, banishing whatever had manifested there to kill those hikers.

They're dead, he realised, and the thought set him running again.

"I don't want to die, I don't want to die," he repeated over and over like a mantra. He hacked at the branches which hung over the track, striking them down like the reaching limbs of monsters. Their spindly fingers caressed his skin, leaving bloody lines in his flesh, death marks to guide others to him. He spun on the spot, surrounded, his weapon held before him like a defensive talisman warding off danger. He panted hard, his lungs ragged, torn sails flapping in the gale of a storm which gusted through him. Sweat mingled with blood, his flesh boiling beneath a paper thin covering of vulnerable skin. He could no longer see the light of the torch, and once more the trail looked like every other trail, seen through a gossamer veil of gloom, the moonlight filtering through the trees, projecting ghostly shapes to further torment his terror-addled mind.

"Hey," hissed a snake, accompanied by a crackle like something moving in dry leaves. He jumped out of his skin, shedding all sense, and set to bashing the ground with his weapon to ward off the viper which he was sure was about to strike.

As he did so, he smelt the stench of death freshen in his nostrils. He was running before he realised it, given new direction by the smell, desperate to be away from it, knowing it must be coming from the site of the massacre back down the trail. But the sickly sweet reek of blood and butchered flesh followed him, as if blossoming anew from gravesite flowers which lined the trail. These bloomed in vivid colours in his mind, born of the sensory overload of the smell striking up through his nostrils and into his brain. They lit the path for him, guiding him even as they sent him mad with fear.

He swung his weapon at these flowers, but this did not banish them. Instead it seemed to make them more vivid, fresh colour and scents wafting up as his strikes passed through them as if through a ghost. The pungent, colourful shapes parted like smoke, only to coalesce again afterwards, becoming denser and thicker in form and olfactory bouquet.

Victor couldn't understand it. It was as if he was carrying death along with him, and no matter how fast he ran, or how much he fought, he could not outpace it or overcome it. Death was his companion, haunting his steps, infecting him. He hugged the object in his hand close to his chest, craving the contact of something solid and reassuring to dispel his fear, but this made everything worse. His fingers felt slimy and cold, clammy as they embraced the thing in his hands. A shiver emanated from it, electrifying his fingers and running through his bones to find the base of his spine. From there the jolt of energy climbed the macabre staircase of his vertebrae, tingling sparks leaping up each step like a slinky defying gravity. When it reached the dizzying heights at the base of his brain, exploding into his skull like fireworks, the true fear manifested into a horrifying realisation.

The object in his hand was the severed leg he'd found.

The reek of death rammed like a spike up through his nostrils and his hands clenched tight like those of a corpse. He wanted to toss the leg away, but he found he couldn't. It clung to him, begging him for help, its ghostly spirit animated by his fear-fuelled imagination. The moon was shining clearer now through a gap in the trees. He could see the pale skin of the leg, smeared with blood, a shattered length of bone protruding from one end of the flesh like a grotesque chicken drumstick.

Victor threw back his head and howled in horror. The sound was taken up by a lone wolf in the distance.

15

"We're going on a monster hunt," sang the pack leader. The Cub Scouts gathered around the campfire echoed the line. They repeated this rhythm of call and answer with the next line of the song. "We're gonna bag a big one."

I hope not, thought Sebastian, tugging nervously at the woggle affixing the scarf around his neck.

"What a sunny day," sang everyone in unison, including Sebastian, because it helped him forget the terrors waiting in the dark night beyond the comforting glow of the campfire.

"I'm not afraid," he said with the rest, the final affirming line of the verse.

But he was afraid. And his mother, Akela, was too busy being the pack leader to all the Cubs, instead of a mother to him, so she did nothing to comfort him as he wriggled and fidgeted his little legs, bringing them close to the fire until they felt scorched and toasted, then drawing them away until he was cold and shivering.

The song went on, with its verses describing the various obstacles to overcome on the monster hunt, whether it was muddy swamp, or a hail storm, or even into the lair of the monster itself. Each time they sang the same refrain afterwards, that they can't go around it, or back the way they had come, only forwards and through. They had to face it head on, no matter what it was or how much they hated the prospect.

The moral wasn't lost on Sebastian. He was smart for an eight year old—too smart for his own good, as his mother never ceased to tell him.

"I'd trade a few points of your IQ to gain you some common sense," she'd say, more often than Sebastian would prefer, as if it were her responsibility to make such decisions if it were possible, and that she would like to design her child to more closely match her expectations.

She smiled at him now as she sang, but she smiled at all the children, and at the moment he was just another of the Cubs, treated with equality, another moral lesson she insisted on instilling in him, here at scouts as much as at school, where he was a student and her a vice principal. There could be no special treatment, not in a public school, not in the boy scouts—these were equal opportunity organisations, sink or swim.

"Uh oh, we've gotta go through it," he sang, thinking of all the years of school ahead of him, all the years of scouts. These were the obstacles standing between him and a life of his own.

But he didn't really want this freedom. Here, in the glow of the fire's circle, in the warm, socially equal embrace of his mother's love, he felt safe. So he turned his back on the darkness which surrounded them, not willing to go through it.

"I'm not afraid," he sang, louder than the others, desperately wanting to believe it.

***

Victor was afraid, more afraid than he'd ever been in his life. He stumbled along the trail like a drunkard, the only thing guiding him gravity, his body weight leaden and dragging him down the side of the mountain to what he hoped was safety. He'd not gotten rid of the leg of the deceased hiker—it was his duty to recover any human remains for a decent burial—but he had wrapped it in a plastic sheet and shoved it in his backpack. It was too big to fit, so it poked out through the zipper, protruding up above his head, making him look like some Frankenstein's monster put together wrong.

He groaned like a zombie, his mind overloaded by horror, his brainless corpse on autopilot, shuffling with outstretched limbs, hoping to reach something which felt warm and soft, a hug from someone he loved to reassure him, tell him there were no monsters out there.

Only there are monsters out here. Something had to have snapped those trees.

He shuddered, the movement shifting the weight of the leg in his pack.

And it ripped the leg off some poor fucker.

He picked up his pace, moving with more purpose, aware he could still be the next victim of whatever was out here killing people. He tried to think, and then not to think, of what exactly it might be. The inside of his skull was a procession of images, the phantasmagoria of vicious and dangerous beasts rearing up in turn then fading, all of them real, living creatures despite their spectral, imagined quality in his mind. He saw bears, wolves, and giant kangaroos. He saw a massive boar with huge tusks and bristling, stiff hair along its spine, and he felt this was the closest and most reasonable guess. The thing that had charged through those trees had the inertia of a truck, and a boar could gore a man to death. But where was the remainder of the corpses? Of two hikers he had only a single leg. The creature—whatever it was—had to have eaten or dragged away the rest of the bodies. That was a lot of flesh, a lot of weight.

It's hungry.

But was its hunger sated? He glanced over his shoulder, saw nothing, and yet he ran as if the thing was right behind him. In his mind it was breathing down his neck, drool dangling, with the hot stink of gore close to his face. The leg in his pack slapped against the back of his head like a terrible reminder of his mortality, goading him on, his terror spiking. He didn't stop until he ran into something hard, a dark mass which reared up out of the night.

***

Sebastian didn't want it to stop. If the singing stopped, then the adults would stare blankly into the fire for a while. Eventually they would slap their knees and say, "Right, time for bed," and the Cub Scouts would be herded off to their tents like sheep into their pens, protected from prowling wolves for the night, but not from the terrors in their own thoughts.

Akela stalked around the perimeter of the Cubs, encouraging them all to sing heartily, to do the accompanying hand gestures which illustrated the songs in physical, symbolic dance like a pantomime for the deaf. Sebastian knew she was trying to wear them out, get them ready for sleep—it was her way of corralling them, carried over from being a vice principal, and to a lesser extent, a mother. But Sebastian was still wide awake, his mind moving too fast so that his body lagged behind. He was doing the movements at the wrong times, throwing everyone out. He was the black sheep, straying from the pack. His mother scowled, annoyed at him, sure this was some type of ploy for attention rather than a manifestation of genuine mental distress. Sebastian couldn't help but project her judgement onto himself, part believing he was making it all up, desperate to stand out.

I want her to love me more than the other kids, he thought. *She's my mother, not theirs. Why do I have to share her?*

But that was just the way it was. Even at home there was his father to contend with, his other siblings, all of them braying like a herd of wild beasts for some piece of his mother, tearing her apart and sharing her out. There was never enough to go around, someone always left hungry, their needs not met. More often than not that was Sebastian—the youngest, the forgotten one, last in line. The one who was too much work, so why bother trying?

"He's being dramatic," they'd say to him every time, calling him Brian Brown, after the Australian actor, like that was some type of universal saying everyone understood and wasn't uniquely used by his family alone, for Sebastian alone.

Sebastian was alone. This was never more in evidence than when the singing ended, the knees were slapped, and everyone headed off to their tents. He was left by himself, left to fend for himself, with only the fire for company, the burning twigs crackling and popping like the distant laughter of the other children as they joked around and readied themselves for a peaceful sleep which would be denied Sebastian.

16

The fire burned down, the last orange embers glowing in their dark casings of cooling black coal and flaking white ash. But the anxiety in Sebastian hadn't been quenched. It roared like a bonfire, stoked by a fear of what lay out there in the darkness.

And there was something there, he wasn't making it up. A she-wolf stalked around the outside of the fire pit, looking in on Sebastian, curious about him, wanting something from him he didn't want to give.

It wanted his whole life.

But this wasn't because this wolf was a predator. It was because she cared for him, and his life was her life, a gift she had bestowed, and therefore had a stake in. Akela, the wolf, the pack leader, loved her son more than the other children. He was her child—it was only natural. But, because it would be so easy to fall into favouritism, she didn't like to show it, because what would that say about her? What would it mean for the other kids, vying for her attention, needing her support to grow?

As a teacher she had a professional responsibility, a stake in their development as well, even though some of these Cubs weren't her students—in fact, most weren't. In this way she was unable to turn off the vice principal in her, and to that part of her were tied her ambitions, her drive, and her goals in life. She couldn't help but act this way, with outwards equality, smoothing out and hiding her own preferences and opinions to provide a universal standard to all.

But—and this was more important to Akela—what would it mean for Sebastian if she showed him he was different? He'd grow up spoiled, or perhaps become more of an outcast than he already was.

She crept quietly towards the dying fire, her mischievous spirit not quenched but enlivened by the night's sing-along. Sebastian, sitting on a log, bristled and went stiff, as if he felt her presence with a sixth sense. He turned his head to the left and then the right, scanning the night sounds with his ears, searching for movement out of the corner of his eyes. Akela shifted her weight silently to remain in the blind spot directly behind him.

Even when he turned around completely he didn't catch her. She froze in place, her green scout uniform blending into trees, nothing but another shadow. He stared right at her, yet couldn't see her. Akela felt saddened by this, misunderstood. She wasn't trying to ignore him. She was trying to teach him a valuable series of life lessons.

Though not right now. Now it was about fun—her fun. She waited for him to twist away from her, back to the fire, and she stalked forward, the silent hunter. Looming over him like a reared up beast he looked small and vulnerable, and she almost didn't pounce.

Almost.

She plunged her arms down, her hands bent, fingers pointed like the fangs of a cobra. She hissed as she nipped him on the shoulders with pinching fingertips. He jumped a foot into the air, springing forward at the same time so that he nearly landed in the smouldering remains of the fire. He shrieked, but these weren't the delighted squeals of playful fear she was hoping for. They were real wails of unfeigned mortal terror. He looked at her with wide-eyed horror, as if she had become the wolf for real, her face grotesquely distorted into a hairy, predacious monster with fangs bared, ready to eat him.

But she wasn't a monster. She was his mother, and she was just trying to have a joke with him, trying to get him to lighten up. Instead, he roused the whole camp with his screams, and she was forced to give him the special attention she so desperately didn't want to. She was particularly galled to do so in front of an audience of curious, impressionable eyes, the other Cubs watching from the flaps of their tents. In the cabins up the hill she knew the adults were judging her, annoyed, storing this piece of information away for later recall and gossip.

This vexed her greatly, because the care she now showed Sebastian was the same she would do for any of the Cubs if they were in distress. Maybe it was his turn, then. This reasoning gave her a way out of her own moral quandary. She softened and became his mother for a little while, putting aside the roles of pack leader and the vice principal. Taking him by the hand, she led him towards her cabin where she could shield him from the darkness of the world.

***

The cabin—that was what Victor had run into. The slap of the impact with the wall was a blow which flattened his nose painfully. He barked a single unintelligible word, more in surprise than pain, and bounced backwards, hands flying to his face. Stumbling and falling, he hit the ground hard and rolled in the dirt. He struggled to rise, his thoughts lost in the tangled maze of a mind made sensitive through long hours spent on edge. His skin felt thin, no protection against the elements, a cool frost in the air, and his nerves jangled back and forth like runaway trains through the subway of his flesh, rattling his bones with their vibrations.

The cabin loomed over him like a monster. It reared up on its hind legs of stilts, the brick chimney a blockish head breathing smoke. Its window eyes shone at him, blank and inhuman, their internal glow the light of an insatiable hunger. The door yawned open like a mouth, its creaking hinges moaning, and something soft and pink protruded from it. It reached for him, an obscene tongue flapping about. Drool fell from it, splashing Victor's face. He sniffed, and the liquid had a pungent chemical smell, the foul stuff brewed in the guts of the monster. His own tongue stabbed at it unconsciously, and he recognised the taste. It was liquor.

The pink protrusion from the door folded back on itself, sloshing the clear liquid back into a mouth within a mouth. Victor's exhausted mind saw a Russian doll inside another, layer upon layer, echoing into eternity. It was a wide abyss opening up to consume him.

A light burst upon his consciousness like a bomb, lighting up the horizon with its atomic explosion. It was red and orange, brilliant yellow, then a flash of white which oozed across the landscape of his soul, a single continuum with the forest around him as it came to life.

For a moment Victor thought a torch was being shone in his face, but no, it was no torch, it was the sun breaking on the dawn, giving all the shapes around him a different mien. No longer was the cabin a monster, nor was its door a mouth, gaping wide to swallow him. And this pink mass was no tongue, reaching out to lick him, but an outstretched hand—a human hand. He took it, and it dragged him up out of the quagmire of his own fear-drenched imagination. He felt lighter immediately, no longer weighed down by the awful thing he had seen in the forest, the evidence of which he carried in his backpack. Instead, he was buoyed up by the round shapes before him, soft and inviting as clouds. He pressed his face into them, and they cushioned his soul, eased the aches in his limbs with their maternal warmth. He was drooling himself now, so relieved and happy to be safe and cared for, his shattered mind regressing all the way back to when he was a baby. He made a cooing sound, reaching with puckered lips for something which was pulled away just as soon as it was offered.

He bawled in offence.

"Can you get your fucking face out of my tits?" said Wright, stepping back from him so abruptly that he nearly fell flat on his face on the cabin's steps.

Victor caught himself, looked up, face flushing red as he realised where he was and what he was doing. He looked around for something, anything to make this better. A bottle of vodka was thrust at him, and he grasped it like a life raft in a turbulent sea. His mouth met the lip of it, and he latched on like a leech, sucking away, unhappy and fussy at first, but quickly soothed into silence by the mother's milk.

"Where the hell have you been?" said Wright, folding her arms across her breasts, as if making it clear they were off limits.

"The hikers," gasped Victor wetly, as if this explained everything.

"I've been calling you on the radio, why didn't you answer?" Wright reached into the cabin, picked up the handset of her radio, and spoke into it. There was a crackle at Victor's belt, her words echoing tinnily through his radio. "You're a wanker," she said, and the insult was repeated in synch at his hip, as if the whole world agreed with her, people crowding around to mock him from every angle.

"The hikers," Victor spluttered between gulps of Vodka.

"What about the hikers?" asked Wright, trying to wrestle the bottle out of his hands. He took another slug of the soothing liquor, desperate to forget even as she tried to dredge the muddy depths of his memory, the squalid pool of the past made murky through alcohol.

"Gone," he managed as his grip slipped on the glass bottle. Wright tucked it protectively between her breasts, held it there like it was her baby.

"Gone where? Left the park?" she asked.

Victor blinked hard, wanting nothing more than to get the bottle back, or else to take its place in that safe space nestled in the valley between two lush hills. But the protection on offer was an illusion, merely a thin veil to pull across the danger to keep it out of sight. Nowhere was safe anymore—there was something out there in the woods, something which killed men, and Victor knew he was nothing but a man, facing an uncaring world full of monsters.

He took a step past Wright into the cabin, preferring to be inside, where there were at least walls to block out the worst of the harsh reality the sun's light had illuminated. He would have thought the dawn a comfort after the ordeal of the long, dark night. But really, it was too much, too revealing. He wanted to forget, to curl up in a hole, bury himself in dirt, safe as a grave, resting in peace, with nothing to worry him, because the worst had already happened—he was dead.

We're all dead, he thought, wondering if he'd ever have the courage to once more go on his usual hikes to patrol the trails and do his daily tasks. This job was his life, but his life was over, ended just as surely as the lives of those kids up on the track. It was only a matter of time. He sensed it in his subconscious, a terror which froze his guts, the alcohol not doing its job. Instead it made reality liquid, so that fear oozed from the walls in crimson streaks.

"What happened to the hikers?" insisted Wright, but Victor wasn't listening. He spun on the spot, jaw hanging open as he watched the walls run with blood. They offered no protection. If trees couldn't stop the beast, what could these flimsy timbers do?

"What's that in your backpack?" asked Wright, a tremor creeping into her voice as she sniffed the air. The ripe stench of death wafted through the cabin.

Victor dropped the backpack, daring her to unwrap the foul package he carried, and fell onto the bed, the room still spinning, his thoughts running around in a circle, goaded by terror. One idea haunted him—that mankind was no longer at the top of the pyramid, no longer the final link in the food chain. This fact alone was clear to him through the haze of alcohol and fear. What he'd seen up on the trail could not be unseen—the thick trees snapped at their bases as if by a hurricane wind, the blood smeared everywhere like a bomb had gone off. It was an inhuman level of destruction. What had done this was no regular beast, no animal of the forest, but something unusual and all the more terrifying in its mystery. Victor knew he'd have to face it eventually—it was his duty to find out what had done this—but he couldn't face it, not yet. And while the cabin was no safe harbour, it was better to be here than out there in the bleak forest, where even the densely packed trees could no longer hide the nightmare they had obscured for so long.

Wright shook him by the shoulders, bouncing him on the bed in angry pantomime of the sex they had earlier.

"Where did that leg come from?" she screamed in his face, confusion mingling with panic in her strangled cry. The comforts of her intoxication had been swept away by the seriousness of the situation.

So she's found it, thought Victor, but he could no longer be drawn on to match her heightened emotions, his wellspring of strong feeling milked dry through the long night of fear. Everything seemed to be happening to someone else far away, a spectacle he watched and could enjoy for its vicarious thrill. This was nothing more than a horror movie or the sport of gladiators in the Colosseum. When it was over he would get up from his seat, return to his life, and once again walk the peaceful trails meandering through the tranquil memory of a national park he loved.

"Where's the rest of this body, Victor? Victor!" cried Wright, pulling him back to reality, reminding him he was submerged in the story, a protagonist rather than a spectator. She was trying to re-infect him with fear.

He started to laugh, a series of burbling sounds rising to manic hysterics. He laughed not because anything was funny, but because he was trapped and didn't know what else to do. He snatched the bottle away from Wright and sought to flee further into himself, the only direction open to him anymore.

17

A door opened for Sebastian, and he walked through it into a new day filled with life, fun, and laughter. The night was the bad time, but it was over. His mother had held him until he slept, easing him with comforting words each time he'd been roused by nightmares, the panic spiking in the moments before he realised she had not abandoned him.

In the morning he found her gone, rising before him to attend to her duties, but by then it didn't matter anymore. He saw the sun's light streaming through the window, and it banished the demons of his mind, evaporating the shadows like rising mist so they could no longer form the shape of monsters in his imagination.

Now there was no more need to think, the day pre-planned by his mother and the other Cub Scout leaders. Activities were laid before him like dishes at a feast, each to be enjoyed in turn, the mind occupied by tasks and puzzles and games, and the body worn out to exhaustion by the same, so that by the time the day was over and the sun was setting, Sebastian had forgotten his fear.

***

Victor woke up and found he had not forgotten his fear. It resided in him like cancer in his blood, spreading to each part of him even as his body tried to heal itself at some cellular level.

He'd slept through the day, the alcohol sinking him so deeply into the mire that Wright had been unable to rouse him. Looking around now, he found her gone. Gone too was the booze, though whether Wright had drunk it, or merely hidden it from him, was unclear.

Getting up wasn't easy, his head heavy and fragile. He balanced it in his hands like an unwieldy yet delicate porcelain vase as he got up to take a leak. The piss was a thin stream of dehydrated brown liquid. He tried to spit into the bowl—his tongue felt furry and tasted awful—but found his mouth dry and sandy as a desert. He downed a glass of water, each gulp like knives in his throat. Stars burst in the corners of his eyes as he went to the window. Even the pale red light of the setting sun was overwhelming. It smeared the trees with the glow of freshly spilt blood, forcing him to remember all he had seen. His limbs shook, the fear mingling with alcohol withdrawal to create a perfect storm of unease.

Desperate for a way out, he conducted a more thorough search for liquor. When he found none, he panicked, his breath sawing in and out of him in ragged gasps. In his mind he was being chased once more, the memories coming for him.

Blood on the trees.

He squeezed his eyes shut, trying to shut out the world, forget the sights he had witnessed. But they followed him into the darkness, sliding through the thin gap of his eyelids like a letter under a door. Written on the pages was a horror story, the night before described as if he were reading a novel. Reliving it all over again reinforced the nightmare quality of the whole ordeal. Fears born of shadows loomed large, creating a picture of what could have possibly smashed those trees, killed the hikers in such a brutal fashion, and taken their bodies away.

He shuddered. They were dealing with something far more awful than a wild beast. There was a monster out there. To him, it was a fact, yet a fact he desperately wanted not to be true, because it undermined his worldview—a vision of life where such things were impossible. He felt dislocated from the past, thrown into a future which led only to death.

Vertigo overwhelmed him. His reality swirled down a plughole. Nausea swelled in his guts and a rising wave of vomit crested in his mouth. Rushing to the sink was pointless, his movements sluggish, the bile surging too quickly. He projectile vomited across the cabin, up the wall. Some of it even landed in the sink—small comfort, as most was a mess on the floor he would have to clean up.

It's always me left cleaning up the mess, he thought, feeling sorry for himself. He tried to scoop the disgusting bile up with his hands, carry it to the sink, but this was futile, and he washed his hands, expunging himself of the responsibility.

Weary of it all, he lay down on the bed, turning his back to the door of the cabin and the world beyond.

***

Sebastian held the world in his hands. It was a small Earth, not spherical, but flat, a mere patch of fabric, with a stitched image of the planet on one side—a conservation merit badge he had earned that day. It meant much more to him than simply its worth as an object, a possession. It was a symbol of achievement and approval. Awarded to him by his mother during the end of day parade, it was everything to him—love, hope, progress, a reason to go on. It took the pressure off for a while. For now he didn't need to do anything to be accepted, he could simply be.

Yet, at the same time, even as it lifted a certain type of burden off his shoulders—the desperate need for validation—it placed another there. Earning a badge was the easy part. Integrating the lessons learned was much harder. To realise the planet was a fragile thing was not easy to understand. That he had a duty to it, even harder. He didn't want that responsibility, not if it exposed him to the source of his fear—the world itself.

The sun was gone. The dark cape of night had been pulled across the national park, and with it, his consciousness grew bleak. Out there, in a world once filled with light and laughter, was now nothing but dread.

He fiddled with the badge as he sat in his mother's cabin. He did not have her permission to be there, but he was pre-empting the future, trying to sidestep the humiliation of begging to be allowed in to sleep at her side, to rest in the light of her warm glow instead of being thrust out into the dark, surrounded by other children in the tents, yet alone, always alone.

The small fabric disk didn't seem like much, but it was all he had to keep him from shaking with fear. It was a life ring, thrown to him in a dark sea, and he clung to it, thinking of the happiness he'd felt as his mother handed it to him on parade, then gave him the three finger scout salute. He'd returned the salute and smiled, happy to be the sole beneficiary of her attention for once, until the next Cub had their name called, and they marched awkwardly with swinging arms across the parade ground to get their own badge. Sebastian always felt betrayed in those moments, as if the badges were meant for him alone. He was good at earning them, and they triggered a dopamine cascade in his brain which kept him happy—but only for a little while, caught in an addictive cycle he was too immature to yet recognise.

Time was running out, the clock on the cabin's wall ticking like a countdown to doomsday. The sound was echoed in the clicking of boot heels on concrete, his mother's steps drawing closer as she walked down the path towards the door. His heart was ticking too, a bomb about to go off in an explosive display of panic to elicit sympathy. The steps stopped outside the door. He was sure she must have seen the light inside. He heard a sigh, saw a shadow cast onto one of the windows, and with it, he felt her disapproval looming like a monster.

In his mind, he saw the smile on his mother's face as she'd handed him the badge, but it was the same smile she favoured all those who got merit badges, and so it melted like wax before the heat of his strong feelings, a burning fire of anxiety the only thing which remained.

He threw the merit badge on the floor, its dopamine all used up, just a useless piece of fabric once more. He needed other stimulus, whether it was love or anger, he no longer cared, as long as he was seen, because that would mean his world was illuminated, the darkness banished for the moment.

The brass knob of the cabin door creaked as it turned.

18

Two doors opened side by side on a split screen, and two women walked through them. They entered cabins not too dissimilar from each other, located on opposite sides of a mountain. The women were not alike in appearance, though they were both middle aged and shared an attitude of annoyed frustration with the person inside their respective cabins—one was a grown man, the other a young boy.

Both the boy and the man were on the women's beds, and while they were different in age, they resembled each other, both having a tangle of brown hair over faces red from heightened emotion. Each also wore a green uniform—that of a Cub Scout or a park ranger—with small, stitched cloth badges sewn onto the fabric. One of these badges lay on the floor. It was mirrored in the other cabin by a patch of cooling vomit. Both these were markers of the petulant dismissal of the world by the man and the boy.

And both were looked on with disapproval by the two women, who slammed the doors in synchronized anger as they stepped into the cabin, making the man jump from the bed in startled terror and the boy to burst into tears. Both the boy and the man were imagining monsters, and neither was going to receive the comfort they longed for from the women.

***

"What are you doing in here?" Akela asked Sebastian, annoyed to find him in her cabin. She frowned in consternation as Sebastian blubbered something incoherent around wracking sobs. Akela watched him in disgust, remaining at a distance.

"You've got to go back to your tent," she said when he'd finally finished trying to choke out words which would not come. This sent him into further hysterics. He tossed himself around on the bed, grabbing the blankets and sweeping them up and over him like waves cresting in a storm, crashing down on him. They provided no real comfort, merely added weight and the illusion of protection. His heart was just as turbulent, the splashes of his tears like the salt spray of a vast ocean, its surface torn to shreds by the violent depths of the emotions hidden below.

"You're being a drama queen," said Akela. She reached forward, and Sebastian threw back the covers to receive her touch, but she bent over and picked up the merit badge he'd thrown on the ground. Without a word, she pocketed it, the love and approval it represented revoked, the past, with all its good behaviour and achievements, swept away by what she perceived as a gross breach of etiquette.

"I thought I could sleep here," said Sebastian in a cold, flat voice, the tears frozen on his cheeks as if in suspended animation, his eyes fixed on the pocket of his mother's trousers into which his hope had vanished. His whole world was in there, encased in darkness, and he wondered if he'd ever get it back, if it would ever see the light of day again.

"That was last night, a one-time thing," said Akela, shaking her head, as if regretting the weak decisions of yesterday and determined not to repeat them.

"You're not going to send me out there," said Sebastian, pointing over her shoulder at something only he could see, a monster glimpsed through the window, with massive, hairy arms, and huge, sharp teeth in a silently roaring mouth.

"I am," she replied, "so out you go."

When he made no sign of moving, she reached out to take a hold of him and pull him out into the cold night. Sebastian saw the hand looming, fingers wide to grasp him, with the palm a dark shadow set to envelop his head. He recoiled from it, seeing in it no love, not even tough love, just cruelty.

"It's out there!" he shrieked, glimpsing the monster once more through the window. It was smashing down the tents and chasing after those who fled from beneath the collapsed folds of canvas. He could hear it now, the roaring reaching his ears like the waves of the impossibly large ocean of emotions in his mind, and maybe even his mother heard it, because she paused for a moment, cocked her head. She shrugged, her electric eel fingers wrapping around Sebastian's arm, sending a jolt of electricity through him, setting his nerves alight with pain and panic.

"No! Let me stay. I thought you loved me," he wailed as she dragged him towards the door. Its blank, wooden face was that of an impassive judge, their gavel hovering to bash him over the head, pronouncing a death sentence.

"I always love you, Sebastian, but sometimes I don't like you," she said. He only heard the second part. To Sebastian it was the executioner's blow, decapitating him, severing all hope. He went limp as a ragdoll in her arms, and she was forced to drag him bodily to the door, which she opened with some awkward juggling.

"Don't do this," he pleaded, not even speaking to her, but instead to the brutally unfair world at large, with its night-time horrors which erased the pleasures of the day. How he wished it was different, but it wasn't. Joy never lasted, and he would be forced to die over and over, the ordeal repeated every night. He was dumped unceremoniously on the porch of the cabin, already an inert corpse with limp limbs, ready to be scooped up and carried away to the carnal pit.

The door closed behind him, cutting him off from his lifeline.

***

"What are you doing in here?" Wright asked Victor. She flicked on a light, filling the cabin with a cool, white fluorescent glow. Victor rolled over on the bed, holding his hands before his eyes to shield them, hissing in pain like a vampire exposed to the sun. He felt like he was melting, his skin waxy and pale as a candle, unable to stand the heat of Wright's presence as she stomped across the room in her heavy boots. The steps rung in his ears like the tolling of a doomsday bell. Each resonating note echoed around his hollow head, building to a deafening cacophony of sound. It built and built into a monstrous roar, so loud he thought he would die.

***

The roar of the monster brought Sebastian back to life. It felt close now, the threat immediate, no longer a far-off thing of his imagination, glimpsed through a window, but alive and real, and deadly close. He sprung up as if electrocuted, his brain a fireworks display of hysterical fear, consumed by colour and explosions of feelings, with no thought, no logic.

He scrabbled at the wooden cabin door, tearing his fingernails but not noticing the pain in his desperation to get back in. Blood ran down his hands, staining the cuffs of his uniform red.

***

"Can you shut the fuck up?" said Wright. It was only then that Victor realised the sound he heard was not her steps, but his own screaming.

19

Screaming filled the Cub Scout camp. Sebastian added to the din himself, mad with terror as he wailed to be allowed inside like a dog in a thunderstorm. His mother ignored him, holed up in the cabin, the door locked. He ran around the outside of the building, banging on the windows, the glass rattling. Still Akela did not come out or even show herself. Instead, she turned the lights off, and it was as if no one was home.

This isn't the time for one of your tough love life lessons, thought Sebastian.

He wanted to yell that there was a monster, a real monster, but she would not have believed him, thinking he was crying wolf. But this time the wolf really was among the sheep. The bleating of the children from the camp was an awful noise of pathetic slaughter, each shrill cry of terror and pain cut off in turn by the meaty thwack of impact from a huge fist pulverising flesh and ending lives. Sebastian forced himself not to look, afraid that if he did, he'd fall on the ground, curl up in the foetal position, and wet himself. He felt strangely sure the reek of his hot piss would draw the monster to him, and he wanted to live, so he instead crawled under the cabin, past its supporting stilts, and buried his head in the sandy soil there.

It did little to muffle the riotous noise of the massacre among the tents, so he looked up—the reality could be no worse than the dread visions his imagination conjured up to accompany the awful soundtrack of death. Dark silhouettes of Cub Scouts and leaders ran across patches of illumination— from the bonfire, from the headlights of a truck, and from a single floodlight on a pole by the mess tent. Added to these were individual torches, which flashed around frantically as the children shone them in every direction, trying to locate the source of their fear.

From his vantage point halfway up the hill, it was easy enough for Sebastian to see it.

One of the silhouettes was far larger than any of the others—a dread monster born of nightmares. It loomed over tents, reaching with long arms to grab at passing children, plucking them like grapes from the vine. One shrieked as the monster caught a hold of them. Sebastian fully expected the thing to throw back its huge head, and with jaws wide open, drop the screaming Cub Scout into its mouth, chomping down with a crunch of bones. Instead, there was a brittle crackle like broken twigs, and a sick squelching like boots in mud as the monster scrunched the child up into a ball like a piece of scrap paper and tossed it over its shoulder.

At first, Sebastian's mind boggled at the mindless destruction of a life, the discarding of the body like trash. The monster was toying with life, uncaring about the brutal consequences of its actions, the ending of a life a mere moment's pleasure, a merit badge tossed on the floor, its usefulness expired. But then he saw the hulking creature repeat the same action again, scooping up another child, who cried pitifully as its legs were snapped forwards at the knees, the elbows snapped backwards, and finally the head folded in like the final loose tab of an origami animal. It seemed such a measured action, so deliberate, and though the monster then threw that child over its shoulder as nonchalantly as the first, Sebastian could see it was not a random toss. The body landed as a tidy bundle beside others to form a pile, and was joined by a steady stream of neatly packaged corpses created by the monster. Sebastian watched this process in horrified fascination.

It's gathering them up. But why?

There could be only one answer. Sebastian felt vomit rise in his mouth, but he swallowed it. The disgusting taste was soured further by the sweet stench of death wafting in the air so that he felt like he had eaten a bit of the rotting corpses himself.

***

"Is this vomit?" asked Wright, backing away from the stain on the cabin's floorboards.

"Yes," said Victor, getting up and staggering to the sink. His mouth tasted like rancid meat. Rinsing it with water did little except dilute the sickly taste and make his tongue feel slimy. "Have you got anything to drink?" he asked without looking up, splashing his face with the water.

"No," said Wright, but he could tell by the way she stepped away from him that she was lying, protecting whatever personal stash she had on her person. "You drunk us clean out."

"I'm sure you helped out a bit," he sneered.

"I don't like your tone."

"Get fucked, how's that for tone?"

"I would have thought you'd have pulled yourself together by now," she said, and went over to turn on the computer, as if she had any intention of doing some work.

"Well, I haven't." He wet a cloth and dabbed at a vomit stain on the collar of his uniform.

"You can't hide from your problem inside a bottle."

"You're one to talk," he said, and looked over to catch her taking a pull on a flask, trying to hide the action behind the ranger's hat she held. Seeing him looking, she sighed and handed it over. He took a pull, felt the gorge rise in his gullet, and quickly handed it back, forcing himself to swallow the foul mixture, pushing it down into the riotous pit of his roiling stomach.

"There's more in the truck anyway," she admitted, not possessing enough willpower to maintain the moral high ground. He looked at her askance, and highly suspected she didn't want to bother sneaking around with her own drinking. That would take effort, and if there was one thing Wright did not like, it was effort.

"You've been into town?" he asked, pushing aside the curtain to look at the truck. It was a dark shadow against even darker shadows. The moon hid behind thick clouds, offering no light, no solace.

"Yeah, where do you think I've been all day?" she said, clicking the mouse of the computer, staring at the screen. The blue glow lit up her round face, making her look like the absent moon, though only a fake version of it, one which held no secrets and illuminated no secret parts of her, nor of anyone else.

"I don't know, making your rounds, checking on the campsites," he said, walking over to her to look over her shoulder. "You know, doing your job."

She scoffed at this, shuffled the mouse around distractedly.

"Something's out there," he continued, "and we've got to make sure people are alright."

"I had something more important to do," she said.

He pointed at the alerts on the screen, the missed calls that had come in from multiple campsites. "More important than this?"

"Mister Responsible now, are we?" she sneered.

"I do my duty."

"Hence all the missed calls."

"Okay, so what were you doing in town?"

"Mailing a package."

"A package?"

"A very important package, if you get my drift." She patted her breast pocket and winked without looking at him.

"I assume you reported the missing persons to the police, though I'm pretty sure they're dead. No one loses a leg like that and doesn't bleed out." He looked about the cabin, and when he didn't immediately find what he was looking for, started a frantic search. "Where's the leg?"

"What do you think I was mailing?" she said.

"The leg? Why the hell would you mail something like that? It's got to go to the police, to the morgue, for Christ's sake! What would possess you to do such a thing?"

"Money," she said with a shrug, as if this was obvious.

Victor's eyes bulged out of his head at that. He was momentarily dumbstruck, his lips moving, but no sound coming out. He coughed, almost threw up again at the spasm of his diaphragm. He swallowed hard, pushing down the lump in his throat so that it splashed down in the mess of his rotten guts.

"Wright," he said, "I don't think you understand. There's some type of monster out there. No regular animal could have done what I saw."

"I'm banking on it," said Wright.

"What the fuck do you mean? Who would pay you for a fucking leg?"

"A bigfoot breeder."

If Victor had been lost for words before, he was something else entirely now, his mind exploding in reverse as the pieces fell into place, forming a hard mass inside his skull which refused to be rattled loose, no matter how much he shook his head in denial.

"Yeah, I reckon we've got a bigfoot on our hands," continued Wright, leaning back in her chair, stretching her arms nonchalantly. "At least I hope so."

"Bigfoot isn't real," said Victor, finally finding the words. He was trying to convince himself, though he second guessed this, as such a creature could explain everything he'd seen up on the trail.

"Of course they're real," said Wright. "Not the first time we've had one, and not the first time I've contacted my friend. He'll pay mega bucks if we have a bigfoot out here."

"What do you mean, not the first time? You've seen a bigfoot before?"

"They're out there. It's a big park, lots of places to hide. And supposedly they hibernate for a long time."

Victor sat down on the edge of the bed. "Wright, if there's a bigfoot out there, aren't you afraid?"

"Oh, terrified, but the money will help me sleep at night, that and the booze in the truck."

"I think I need a drink," said Victor, heading for the door.

"Easy there, you don't want to let it get on top of you, trust me on that. Either you use the drink, or the drink uses you."

"I feel like I'm going insane."

"You've been through a bit of an ordeal. I feel for you, buddy. I really do. But you're better off facing this thing head on. Don't worry, you'll get your cut."

"I don't want a cut! It's blood money."

"Blood money?" snorted Wright. "Don't be ridiculous."

"Are you thick in the head or just blinded by greed?" asked Victor. "We've already got two dead people out there. You think the monster is going to stop at that?"

"I see no reason—"

He cut her off with a jab of his finger, pointing at the computer screen, at the number of missed calls, from not only the ravers, but from the Cub Scout troop on the far side of the mountain as well. "Kids, Wright. There are kids out there."

Wright shook her head and said, "So, what are you going to do? Go run around the park, get yourself killed?"

"They deserve to be warned about the bigfoot."

Wright gave a long whistle as she used the mouse to scroll through the distressing number and frequency of missed calls he'd slept through. Victor hurried over to the radio. It was off, so he turned it on, dialled through the channels until he heard screaming cutting through choppy static.

"I got a feeling they already know," said Wright.

20

"Where are you going?" Wright asked Victor as he pulled on his jacket.

"To save those Cub Scouts," he said. "Give me the key to the gun safe."

"You going to put them out of their misery?"

"If there's a bigfoot out there, I'm going to shoot it, put an end to this."

"Then, no, I'm not giving you the key."

"Why the hell not?"

"I told you I got a bigfoot breeder coming in. And they'll not pay for a dead bigfoot, will they?"

"We can't just sit here while it's killing people."

"I can and I will. I go out there and suddenly I'm the people it's killing."

Victor hesitated. He didn't want to relive the horror of the trail—the mortal terror of feeling like a monster was chasing him. Even the memory of it was enough to make him shuffle back from the door. He felt the subterranean tug of his soul towards the bottle, the easy way out. He didn't want to die.

But there are kids out there.

He squeezed the bridge of his nose, conflicted, angry at himself for being such a coward. His hangover was killing him, and the pain was a poignant reminder of what he could expect as a reward for any heroics, his body smashed apart into its constituent pieces by an awesomely powerful monster, just to end up bagged up and posted off as further evidence of the bigfoot's presence.

He opened his eyes, blinked away the starbursts, and glared daggers at Wright. She had a wry smile on her face, as if by his dithering he was proving the strength of her cynical worldview.

"Take the money, look the other way, and have a drink to forget about any niggling doubts," she said, summing up its main points.

Yes, forget. I so desperately want to forget, thought Victor. *The only problem is I can't.*

"I don't want the money, and I can't look the other way," he said. "And if you think drink will clear your conscience, you're an idiot."

"Maybe not clear, though it will ease it a little bit." She produced her flask, raised it in cheers, and drank.

"And what will happen when the authorities find out we didn't report this?"

Wright smacked her lips. "We'll report it in due course."

"It'll be too late then."

Wright leaned over to the radio, the crackling static still interspersed with screaming. She switched it off, silencing the cries. "It's too late already. They're dead."

"They've got the timestamps on those phone calls," he said, pointing at the computer.

"Phone calls *you* failed to answer, I might add. Like it or not, you're in this thing." She used the mouse to select the call logs in question. "Tell you what, I'll do you a favour and let you off the hook."

"Don't," said Victor, his conscience gnawing at his brain. It was overridden by the power of his hangover, pounding like a judge's gavel. Powerful forces were at war inside him, his head versus his heart. Yet he knew one thing for sure, he didn't want to go to jail, held responsible for negligence, and so he did nothing as Wright's finger hovered over the keyboard like the sword of Damocles.

"Don't what?" she said, letting the finger fall, hitting the delete key. The call logs disappeared. "All quiet on the Western front, as far as we're concerned, eh?"

Victor let out an involuntary sigh of relief. Wright smiled at this, vindicated and happy. She leaned back in her chair, grasped her own breasts contentedly. They looked heavy and full in her hands. Victor wanted a drink. He glanced at the door and the truck beyond, laden with liquor. He shook his head.

"But damn it, we can still do something," he said.

Wright let her breasts drop. "I've done all I plan on doing, and if you want to go running around out there, get yourself killed, that's your business."

"Keys to the gun cabinet," he demanded, extending a palm. She shook her head slowly, eyes fixed on his. Victor closed his hand into a trembling fist. "Fuck you, Wright, you utter piece of shit! You're letting those people die. You might as well have killed them yourself."

"The bigfoot killed those people," she said. "All I've done is not be one of them."

"You're profiting off their deaths."

"At least some good will come of this."

"*Good?*"

"I know you've got all these high ideals about being a park ranger, Victor. But stop for a second and see reason. You can take the money and live or you can go out there and die for nothing."

"And what if I go to the authorities, tell them everything?"

"We both know you're not going to do that. You're up to your neck in it already."

"Maybe I deserve to be punished then." He reached into his shirt's collar, fished out the cross on its chain.

"We're all sinners, Victor," said Wright with a sneer. "You're not special just because you think Jesus is watching."

"Yes, he is watching, and that's why I have to go save those Cubs."

"I'm not letting you in the gun cabinet. You'll blow your own foot off."

"I'm taking the truck."

"Can't let you take the truck, Victor. They'll dock my paycheque if you wreck it."

"Bet you left the keys in the ignition though, right?"

She slammed the front legs of the chair down in response, her face serious now. She made a move for the door, but Victor was already through it, grabbing the bear spray and the heavy Maglite as he went. He jumped in the truck, slammed the door in Wright's face. She scrabbled pathetically at the window.

"At least leave me a bottle, you mad bastard!" she cried. The pained look on her face steeled Victor. Her skin was slack like melted wax, horribly distorted by her desperate addiction, the corners of her mouth and eyes dragged down by invisible hooks. It was like looking into a horrible mirror of the future, and Victor didn't want to end up like that.

The bottles of booze jiggled in a box in the backseat as he started the truck and turned it around, playing a tinkling melody of bright angelic notes. His hangover distorted this into a jarring cacophony of brittle, painful sounds, making it much easier to ignore this siren's song.

I'm not taking the easy way out anymore, he thought as he aligned the truck down the road like a compass needle pointing true north. His course was set, his fate sealed. He was heading towards danger, regardless of the consequences. If he didn't die trying to help, he wouldn't be able to live with himself.

***

"Where are you going?" Sebastian shouted in distress, seeing his mother burst from the cabin door and fly down the porch steps.

"To save my Cubs!" Akela called over her shoulder, not looking back.

She's abandoning me, thought Sebastian. *She only cares about them, not me.*

She was sprinting towards the monster and Sebastian felt like he was watching a car crash in slow motion, the deadly result inevitable. His whole world collapsed, reality folding in on itself to form the horrifying pattern of a new life without his mother. It was not a future he wanted to face, and this fear was stronger than that of any monster.

He got up and ran. He headed towards the monster, chasing the thing he wanted to protect—his mother—though he had no idea how he was going to do so. He got a glimmer of what it must be like for Akela as pack leader, responsible for all those young and helpless lives, caring for them and looking out for them. He felt selfish for trying to monopolise her love, which he realised must be much more expansive than his own, able to hold not only him in its warm light, but all these other children as well.

She was throwing herself into danger like a fierce lioness, screaming defiance and waving her arms to draw attention away from the remaining Cubs, who scattered into the forest in all directions. And while the monster was fast—its long legs carried it swiftly after each of its prey—it could not get them all and some slipped through its grasp and escaped into the trees like frightened hares.

"Over here, you big lump!" shouted Akela. She had a bulky yellow waterproof torch in her hand, the beam of bright light waving around, drawing the monster's attention. It huffed at her with a derisive snort and didn't take the bait. Instead, it knocked over a tent with a backhanded slap, revealing a huddle of Cub Scouts trembling like a set jelly. The monster cupped its enormous hands around the children, lifting them up and squeezing them together into a ball of flesh. It twisted its grip, wringing the blood out of the bodies like a wet sponge. It fell in a dark rain onto the white tent canvas.

Sebastian quailed at this horrifying sight, but kept going, drawn like a magnet to the iron of his mother. She was not fleeing, slowly yet stoically walking towards the monster, her steps leaden with her own fear. Sebastian reached her and grabbed her around a leg, hung there like a baby koala, weighing her down further, begging her to stop.

"Run, Sebastian!" she said through clenched teeth, voice strained. Her face was red with stress. A vein on her temple pulsed with heavy heartbeats. Her breathing was shallow.

"I'm not letting go," said Sebastian, clinging tighter.

"Do as you're told. There's no point in us both dying."

"I don't want either of us to die!"

But that wasn't in their hands. It was in the hands of the monster. And it loomed over them, having dispatched all other available prey. Akela swung the beam of the torch up beneath her chin, illuminating her face from below as if she were back around the campfire, telling a spooky story.

This was no story. This was real.

The monster squared up to Akela like a fighter sizing up its opponent, sensing the dignity and defiance radiating from her. Sebastian saw the creature clearly as the beam of light in his mother's hand dipped forward in awed respect like a bowing courtier. Its face was almost man-like, yet grotesquely ugly with cartoonish distorted features, framed by thick brown hair, stiff like the bristles of a broom. This hair covered a body far more muscular than the biggest of bodybuilders, and towering tall, so that Sebastian had to crane his head to stare into the bulbous eyes, which looked like red-speckled eggs nestled in heavy brows. He saw a grim intelligence there. The staring eyes were those of a hunter focused on their prey.

He felt a flash of telepathic communion between himself and the beast, and he willed it to spare him and his mother, but he got the response he expected, or at least imagined.

I have to do this, it said to him with those determined eyes.

Sebastian thought his reply. *But why?*

The only response he got was the monster raising its massive fist. It hung there, as if the monster might reconsider, but then dropped like a heavy boulder. It punched down into Akela's body, which was not made of iron after all, only fragile flesh which exploded under the impact and drenched Sebastian with blood.

21

Victor clenched his teeth, fighting the steering wheel as he took a sharp corner of the dirt road far too fast. His headlights danced around like wild, frightened eyes, scanning the forest all around as he went over bumps and swerved around bends. The engine of the truck roared like an angry beast, and Victor's heart beat loudly in his ears like thumping footfalls. The combined effect excited his imagination, took him back to a place in his mind where the monster was chasing him, gaining on him despite the speed of the truck. He slammed his foot down harder. The engine screamed shrilly, and he felt a thrill, as if he'd driven a spear through the beast's heart, killing the thing.

But he knew it wouldn't be so easy in reality. He looked at the torch and the bear spray bouncing about on the seat next to him. They seemed pitiful weapons, and he wondered if this mad rush to the Cub Scout campsite was worth it, if he could actually help. What did he hope to achieve?

If I can save one life, I'm willing to risk it.

But what if, instead of saving a life, he lost another—his own. He didn't want his own corpse added to the pile of the dead.

No more time to think, the decision already made as he drove through the wooden arch of the camp's gate. He'd built that gate himself, hung the letters of the camp name on the crossbeam. They spelt a name of doom, and he prayed to Jesus they wouldn't be the site of his grave.

Death was not elusive. It rushed up at him quicker than he thought possible. A ghoulish sight greeted him in the camp as he drove between rows of flattened tents. Smashed and broken corpses, their twisted limbs folded inwards to form bundles of flesh, were piled in a makeshift cairn in the middle of the road. He yanked on the steering wheel to avoid this grim obstacle, but he'd reacted too late. The truck's bull bar struck it like a wrecking ball as he ploughed through in an explosive spray of gore. Victor wailed in terror as he saw heads and limbs bounce up and over the truck's bonnet, others hurled out to the side like macabre Halloween candy thrown from a parade day float. A huge spray of blood slapped into his windshield, obscuring sight like a splash of red paint. His knee-jerk response was to hit the windshield wipers, but this only spread the mess about, and the wipers got jammed against a child's head, which slid back and forth, squeaking obscenely at him as the dead skin wiped the glass like a squeegee.

He slammed on the brake. The truck skidded to a halt, sliding sideways into a pole with a floodlight atop it. The pole toppled over and the light smashed on the ground and went out. The truck's engine stalled and conked out, lurching forward a foot then settling, like a beast shot through the heart taking its last step before weakening, slumping to the ground to die.

An eerie silence dominated the night air, the only sound being Victor's heavy breathing, whistling in his ears. It had a ghostly quality, the impression made stronger by the steam rising from the engine, wafting in banks through the illumination of the headlights as Victor peered into the red smeared mess on his windshield. The child's head looked back at him with blank, staring eyes, and this made him jump, but he dared not make any more noise.

He froze, fear taking a hold, heightening his senses. He strained to hear any sound, simultaneously willing his heart to slow so that its pounding wasn't so loud in his ears. Through the deathly silence he could make out a far off noise—the panicked cries of children running in the woods. They sounded as if they were already dead, spectres haunting the forest, calling him to join them.

He shook his head to deny their pleas. He wasn't getting out of the truck.

Terror closed around him like fog, making everything seem hazy. But he remembered why he'd come. And it wasn't to cower inside the truck in fear, but to save those children. He reached over and grabbed the Maglite in one hand, the bear spray in the other, turned the torch on with a shaking thumb, switched off the spray's safety with the other.

The beam of white light from the torch soothed his horror-riddled mind for a second as he hugged it close. Then he heard a shuffling noise in the gloom beyond the headlights. He shone the torch out the window and nearly jumped out of his skin as he realised he'd narrowly missed hitting another one of those disgusting corpse piles. Steam rose from the tangled mass of gore, bones, and faces. The fear came screaming back at him, tearing through his soul like a howling wind, making him shiver in its cold embrace. Glittering orbs caught the light of his torch, the wet eyes of the dead glistening like those of fish in the marketplace.

He swallowed hard through a throat suddenly dry, and his stomach churned like a cement mixer, its contents gritty and sludgy. The smell of the corpses made him feel like their putrid flesh was in his bowels, and his sphincter loosened at the thought, emitting a wet fart of terror which sounded far too loud in Victor's ears.

Like a single moving stone triggering an avalanche, his flatulence set something in motion which made him nearly shit himself. A monstrous roar bellowed off to his right, beyond the pile of corpses. He instinctively swung the beam of the torch at a flicker of movement, naively thinking the light would scare away whatever made that horrible sound. He caught a glimpse of an ape-like face twisted in anger, great fangs bared, pink tongue warbling in its throat as it bellowed its bestial war shout.

Victor's heart turned to ice. The bigfoot was real.

He could only respond with a bark of surprise and shock, the pitiful, strained squeaking noise lost in the auditory barrage of the bigfoot's cry as it charged. With a deafening bang, it collided bodily with the truck like a footballer making a tackle. The whole truck slid sideways a few metres. Victor reflexively squeezed the trigger of the bear spray, unintentionally gassing himself in the truck's compartment. He spluttered and coughed, dropping both the objects in his hands. They skittered and bounced around as, with a sound of tortured, tearing metal, the truck tilted over at an alarming angle. Victor had no choice but to reach out and brace himself as the truck was flipped over by the bigfoot's massive strength, landing on its side with a clattering bang.

Dazed and confused, his eyes red and burning, and still struggling to breathe, Victor fought in the tangle of his seatbelt. He was unable to see much, but it was clear the monster was still out there—it was bashing the truck with its wrecking ball fists, the clanging impacts playing havoc on Victor's headache, making him wince with pain and fumble with the seatbelt's release.

He finally got himself free of the thing, and was rewarded for his success by a fall down across the passenger seat to slam hard into the door touching the ground. He cursed, but quickly stopped when he realised the noise set the bigfoot into a more frenzied effort to smash its way into the truck. It grabbed the chassis and shook violently, rattling Victor's poor tortured head, scrambling his brains.

At least he found the Maglite, but this drew more attention, as it was still on. So he used it to locate the bear spray and then turned it off. The torch was now nothing but a metal club, and it felt a meagre weapon in his hand. While it was heavy enough to crack the skull of a man if swung hard, he doubted it would do much against that monster, so he dropped it, grasping the bear spray with both his trembling hands.

The bigfoot wasn't giving up. It was pushing the truck, shunting it sideways. After a few metres progress, it growled angrily, and Victor quailed as the monster lifted the truck. It lurched at an angle and went over once more, sending Victor bouncing around the cabin. He'd managed to shift his grip so he didn't spray himself again, and he wondered if the stuff would have any effect on such a big creature.

I sure hope so, he thought, as he looked out the window and saw something which goaded him to action. The bigfoot was pushing the truck onto a big, burning bonfire. With a huge heave, the vehicle tumbled over into it, landing with a spray of sparkling embers thrown up into the dark sky. Fire and smoke immediately filled the truck's cabin. Victor had no choice, he had to get out. Lashing out with a boot, he kicked open the truck's glass sunroof, went through this makeshift escape hatch. He rolled through the flames, scorching his clothes and searing his skin painfully. He kept rolling as he hit the grass, both to extinguish his smouldering clothes and to put some distance between him and the bigfoot.

But the distance shrunk to nothing as the monster took two long strides. It punched downwards into the ground, right where Victor had been a split second before, leaving a deep imprint in the dirt. For something so big the thing was quick and Victor couldn't get away, because even as he scrambled to his feet and ran, it lashed out with a simian arm, caught his foot and tripped him. He fell forward and slid painfully across the stony road.

Roaring in triumph, the bigfoot leapt into the air, a silhouette arcing across the light of the bonfire like a blazing comet. With an earth-shaking impact, it landed astride Victor, huge feet pulverising the road either side of his head. It had missed him by inches, toying with him.

It could have mashed me to paste with its weight, thought Victor, his whole body turning to jelly in fear as he stared up at the thing. Its legs were stout columns rising to a statuesque monolith of a body, broad chested and powerful as a gorilla. The dense covering of dark brown hair made it resemble a totem pole carved out of wood by indigenous people. Time slowed, and Victor saw his death in that perfect shape, a bestial form conjured by the devil to haunt man. He muttered a prayer to Jesus to deliver his soul to heaven, and clenched his fists, bracing himself for the hammer blow which would crush his skull, end his life.

The squeezing of his fingers set off a spurt of the bear spray he'd somehow kept a hold of—the jet of pungent spray struck the bigfoot in the matted hair of its leg. The monster recoiled instinctively from it, wrinkling its huge nostrils as it sniffed the air with displeasure. With a sudden jolt it doubled over and sneezed, the sticky splat of webbed mucus striking Victor square in the face. Terrified and blinded, he activated the spray again, sweeping the nozzle back and forth. He felt the bigfoot back off, its huge feet slapping the ground, and heard it coughing and spluttering.

With his free hand Victor dragged at the gloopy snot which coated his face, tearing it off like a green rubber mask. He immediately wished he hadn't, for what he saw was a primordial horror born in the ancient times of Earth's distant past. The enraged bigfoot glared at him, its reddened eyes dark blood clots. Hate radiated off the monster like heat from the bonfire at its back. It breathed in and out in short huffs, stopping and starting, as if the air itself was its enemy, and shook its head angrily, annoyed that its toying with Victor had been checked by the spray.

But now the games were over, this time it would kill him, Victor was sure of it, his death not a threat but a promise as the monster took a menacing step forward, a growl rumbling in its throat. Far off, beyond the treeline, the children still screamed as they ran, and Victor took some solace in the fact he'd given them a bit more time to get away.

At least I did something useful before the end, he thought, and he felt tears well in his eyes. He hoped it was enough to redeem his soul.

"I'm a sinner, and I'm sorry. Jesus forgive me," he said.

The bigfoot grunted once like an executioner saying 'enough,' bringing an end to the condemned person's final words. The monster did not charge, it took another step forward and struck down, its flattened hand acting as the heavy blade of a guillotine to chop Victor's head off.

Victor tried to accept his fate, but his body rebelled, fighting for life on an instinctual level. He squashed his head down into his shoulders and the bigfoot's karate chop sliced into the ground rather than through his neck. It let out an angry bellow and raked its hand through the dirt, scooping Victor up in its huge palm. He wriggled and writhed in its grasp as the meaty fingers closed around his waist like a vice, threatening to squeeze him like a tube of toothpaste, his head popping off and his guts erupting out of his neck. The pain was excruciating as the pressure increased and Victor emitted a strangled squeak of terror, sure his life was about to end in agony. He flailed uselessly with his arms as the bigfoot lifted him close to its face to inspect him closely, and he had a strange thought that the thing was curious about the unique trait of this human which had held it at bay with its repellent gas emissions.

The bear spray. Oh, good lord Jesus, the bear spray, thought Victor as the bigfoot tightened its grip, crushing his lungs like a boa constrictor. His head swam, his vision turning grey from a lack of oxygen. With the last of his strength he angled the nozzle of the spray canister up towards the looming face. He squeezed the trigger, baptising the bigfoot with a blast which went directly into its eyes and nostrils. The monster spasmed and its head bucked back as if struck by a powerful blow. Victor shrieked with pain as its grip went tighter for a moment, then he was falling, dropped as the huge hand slackened its hold. He fell in the dirt, gasping for air and clutching his torso. His lungs felt flattened and struggled to fill, each breath shallow and laced with tiny needles which tore up his insides.

The bigfoot was no happier, wracked by a coughing fit and sneezing violently. It danced about from foot to foot, nearly crushing Victor as it scratched at its face, desperate for relief from the burning sensation of the capsaicin in the spray. Desperate for some distance, Victor kicked and scrabbled away a few metres while it was distracted, and then gave it another blast as he struggled to his feet, driving it back towards the bonfire. Emboldened, and high on adrenaline, he took a step forward, and another, sweeping the spray back and forth before him. The bigfoot bawled like a distressed baby, tears streaming from it eyes, drool dangling from its lips as it coughed and choked.

Fleeing the spray, it stumbled blindly into the fire, its feet throwing up a wave of burning embers. The bigfoot jumped into the air, bellowing in pain and frustration. Victor tried to get it to fall backwards into the fire by spraying it again, but the spray spluttered and ran out. He looked at it in mute despair, and his first thought was that Jesus had abandoned him. His own hubris had caused him to overreach, and now he backed away, sure the tables had turned once more and the bigfoot would reach out and crush him. But the monster was too caught up in its own distress, howling in agony. The flesh of its feet was charred and blackened, the skin sloughing off, and its face was inflamed as if suffering from a terrible allergic reaction.

The bigfoot shot Victor a final angry glare. It barked a single grunt and turned away, running from him. Heading towards the treeline, it paused only to scoop up one of its piles of corpses, like a thief caught in the act, making off with what they could carry.

Victor made the sign of the cross with the bear spray and let the empty canister fall to the ground. The bigfoot fumbled with its awkward burden and dropped something as it fled, disappearing into the forest as fast as it could run. Victor limped over, grasping his bruised sides, praying for a miracle. He reached the thing on the ground—a human body, that of a young boy. He reached down to touch the face, so serene it seemed the boy merely slept.

But no, that was impossible. The boy's arms had been snapped off at the shoulders, the stumps oozing blood, and the little legs were bent upwards so far the feet touched his chest. He was dead, and Victor grieved for him as if he were his own son, although he had no children and doubted he ever would.

If only I got here sooner, he thought, scratching at the skin of his cheeks in grief and self-condemnation. *If only I hadn't gotten so drunk.*

The screaming from the forest grew louder, children fleeing out of it instead of further in as the bigfoot crashed through the trees. They converged back towards the campsite, a ragged horde of terrified youth. There were no adults among them, and Victor wondered absently if they'd all been slaughtered trying to defend the kids. He realised how lucky he had been himself.

Maybe Jesus hasn't abandoned me after all, he thought, but he couldn't be so sure, the vision of hell crowding in around him, chunks of human bodies scattered about, covered in blood which glistened in the soft glow of embers scattered from the bonfire.

Yet some still live.

The children's eyes were hollow and sunken with the exhaustion of terror. Their skin shone glossy with fear sweat in the moon's light. A half of each of their faces was lit by the flickering flames of the bonfire, animating their anxious features, the other half hidden in shadow, a part of them forever extinguished by what they had witnessed—life now demarcated into light and dark, the black void of death always looming, having been made manifest in the form of the bigfoot.

Those children had been forced to grow up that night, the horrible truth of omnipresent looming disaster made apparent. They weren't safe, never had been, nor would they ever be safe again, not truly, not if something like this could happen here. Their youth, their innocence, was shattered, unable to be put back together. The thin illusion of fun drawn across the camp was gone, torn violently away and replaced with the macabre memory of what they'd witnessed. Victor felt his heart go out to them. He wanted to protect them, but there was little he could do, and even less that could be done about the trauma that had been written on their hearts in hot blood.

But the future is something else, he thought. *I can still help make things a little better.*

He was shaking all over as he grabbed the edge of a downed tent. He pulled the huge canvas across a bloody mess of scattered corpses, obscuring them like a sculptor whose masterpiece wasn't ready for the eyes of others.

If only I could forget the sight so easily.

This seemed to calm the Cub Scouts a little, and a few of them even helped with the next tent. They cried as they tugged at the canvas, obscuring the past with that thin veil of fabric. It did nothing to hide the charnel house stench.

Soon most of the bodies—and scattered body parts—were hidden, but there was presently little they could do about the blood soaking into the dirt road and spattered across the grass in glossy smears. It caught the light of the bonfire, dancing red like a sunset, and Victor knew something had ended, a part of his soul disappearing behind a horizon he hadn't known was there. He breathed heavily, and this had a bad effect on the Cub Scouts, who looked to him for guidance. They saw his rising panic and mirrored it, fretting and wringing their hands, rocking on the spot, curled into balls, tears omnipresent, streaming down faces distorted by anguish.

Victor clutched at his chest, caught the cross dangling there. He sought comfort from it, squeezing it hard, as if it were his heart he was constricting, forcing it to beat less frantically. The metal points of the cross bit into his hand—the sharp pain focused Victor's reality far too much, making everything seem jagged and pointy. He released the cross as if rejecting its promise of salvation through the bloody torture of crucifixion. He didn't want more pain, didn't want to be transformed. His senses were cranked up too high, and everything hurt—he needed the agony of existence to ease up.

I could really use a drink, he thought, taking an unconscious step towards the bonfire and its bright yet deadly flames, attracting him like a moth, leading to his destruction. The truck was ablaze, a wreck flipped on its side. It was smashed and battered, the panels dented and metal torn as if it had been involved in a crash with a heavier vehicle.

Head on with the bigfoot, thought Victor, still walking towards it, heedless of the danger. The alcohol had been in the backseat, and he knew the bottles would be broken.

Maybe there's still one intact. I only need one. A single drink, and I'm done.

But it would never end with one. One would become two, and two would stretch into infinity. If he gave in now the terror would win. He would never be able to face the horrible reality of life sober again.

As if his own soul—or perhaps the power of Christ—were at work, the truck went up in an expansive whoosh of flames. It didn't explode, but the fuel tank had caught, and now the bonfire and the truck were one, an immolated mass of roiling fire and charred metal. For a second, Victor considered throwing himself onto the pyre—a pagan funeral to end his suffering—but instead he patted the cross at his chest gently, soothing himself and reassuring Jesus that he was still on his side.

He turned his back on the blaze to find the eyes of the children staring up at him. The wide orbs glittered expectantly, looking to him for comfort and direction. For a brief, blissful moment, Victor felt like this was a normal visit to the camp, one where he would stand in front of groups of youths such as this and speak on the danger of bushfires, the need to pick up litter, or about trees and their life cycles.

He frowned down at those weary, fearful faces, and couldn't help but think this was the end of one cycle and the beginning of another for all of them. He and all these Cubs would never be the same again. Their past selves were as dead as the bodies under the canvases, or those the bigfoot had carried away.

Victor grimaced, wondering what the monster intended to do with them. He took in a deep breath, the bloody stench reminding him of a trip he'd taken to a slaughterhouse as a child. He'd never banished the sight of the cow hung upside down by its legs, its throat cut so that its head hinged back like a trapdoor, blood gushing out in a cascade like water through an open sluice. He looked at the children around him, could picture the same happening to them, and he realised with distaste that they were simply food to the bigfoot, meat to be butchered. He saw their heads fold back like flapping mouths howling in pain, geysers of blood shooting forth in an arcing spray of heavy droplets like so many tears. The liquid speckled daintily on his face, so delicate, a harvest of pain transmuted from lost life force. He licked it. It tasted fresh and clean. He smiled as he swallowed the fluid.

It was rain, normal rain. He looked up at the gathered clouds obscuring the moon so that the only remaining source of light was the bonfire. The shadows deepened all around to swallow him and the children like the hungry mouth of the monster. A dread chill ran down Victor's spine, making his limbs shake like those of a limp puppet. He had to fight to gain control of himself once more, his nervous system sluggish to respond as if it no longer wished to obey his commands. He felt detached from his body, a defence mechanism, and his mind floated freely among the dark clouds in the sky, merely watching the events below instead of participating in them. This allowed him to function, reality obscured under a veil of delusion.

"Come on, Cubs," Victor said using his friendly park ranger voice. "Let's get one of these tents set up."

The children responded to this small kindness as if they were seagulls thrown a scrap of food. They squawked and flapped about, bunching in close around him so he could barely move. They pecked and tugged at his clothes and his flesh, until he felt like the victim of a pack of scavengers, such was their desperation for any morsel of love and attention. He had to fight his way through them, patting heads and doling out soothing words like thrown breadcrumbs, greedily gulped down by the Cubs, more and more asked of him as soon as he thought he was done.

With them latched onto his legs and arms it took him a while to find a tent which didn't contain some scene of atrocity. When he did, he had to peel the Cubs off him like leeches. He set them to work, and they were keen for the distraction, so the huge tent, a mess tent of old khaki green canvas, went up quickly. With the task complete, the Cubs milled about, lost, as did Victor for a while. He wanted to call for help, but the radio had been in the truck.

Even if I got Wright on the horn, she wouldn't come, he thought bitterly. He was alone. The Cubs didn't feel like people. They were kids, no one he could talk to, and he was afraid to say much, because he feared if he did he would tear the scab off the wound of their recent trauma and a river of tears and wailing would be his reward. Instead, he found a camp chair, put it in the middle of the tent, and sat down as if he were about to begin story time. But he held no book, nor was there a thought in his head he could convey, even' to distract them all.

The Cubs huddled around him as if he were a source of light and warmth. But he was just as cold as them, just as despondent. He looked at the bonfire through a tent flap with glazed over eyes, the flame reflected in those glassy orbs, giving the illusion of animation in his soul, which now felt dark, hollow, and lifeless.

There they waited for either morning or death, the silence only broken by the crackle of flames and the occasional sob of the children.

22

Sebastian was not dead, though he wished he was. The agony he felt was acute, his arms and legs broken, his body stiff, the angles and form all wrong, that of an abstract sculpture rather than a living boy. His mind was similarly destroyed, shattered by trauma both physical and mental, his brain a hard lump sunk into the base of his skull. Blinded by pain, he was cut off from regular thought, the neurons firing against blank walls, unable to penetrate the shock his body had deployed to save him from the worst of his horrific ordeal.

His mother was dead. This was the one thing which remained in his mutilated mind, though it was more an emotional impression than a thought, a memory tied up in a series of visceral images which had scarred his soul. They were like ink patterns in a Rorschach test, and their significance was more about what they meant to him than what they actually were. He saw violence, loss, and terror—the ending of his world. She had been everything to him, and now she was gone.

The wrecking ball fist of the monster had crushed the life from his mother. It had descended fast as a lightning bolt, sending a seismic shudder through her body which knocked Sebastian out. A small mercy, though one which could not last—his consciousness jumped forward to a time of future horror. He'd awoken in terrible pain, his face greasy with viscous blood. The monster huffed and puffed somewhere above him, its heavy footfalls pounding fast like a drum below. There was little light, a slither of the moon visible, the silver slicing across his vision like a threatening blade. He saw by this wan light that his mother's pulverised body had been scooped up with his own and carried away by the monster. Her smashed head was close to his, bumping against his face, her rigid, cold lips giving him a goodnight kiss on his forehead, preparing him for the eternal rest which awaited him.

Sebastian wanted to scream, but couldn't, his lungs tight with fear. He knew any sound would alert the monster. Perhaps that would be a mercy. If it became aware that one of its meat parcels was alive, the monster could end this nightmare with a squeeze of its powerful arms. Instead, frozen in terror, Sebastian waited to see what happened as the beast ran on, cradling the mass of corpses in its arms as if they were its babies.

***

Sebastian woke in panic, not having realised he'd fallen asleep. Perhaps he'd passed out from pain and shock, his body providing the only relief it could. The agony came rushing back over him in a wave, his mind spiking with sensations too hard to integrate into a sane reality. He almost moved in an unconscious response, a desperate need to stretch out his tortured limbs reflexively shoving its way into his forebrain, but he couldn't. A phantom spasm ran down his spine, nerves sending messages out to parts of his body which didn't respond. The signals bounced back as if they'd hit a brick wall, and they bunched up in Sebastian's mind, adding to his confusion, making his panic spike further.

He was paralysed.

At least he was still breathing, though he took little solace in this. He could only take shallow gasps, the fear closing in on him as much as the disgusting corpses all around him. He saw them more clearly now, their wrecked faces surrounding him like an array of broken puppets. They leered with blank, plastic-like eyes, staring and unblinking. Worst of all was his mother. Her torn features, distorted and ripped, were bruised a deep purple. Her eyes held no spark of life. They were dead fish eyes, glossy like a child's marbles, and yet they contained a message of condemnation, as if she blamed him for their predicament.

I can't save you, Mum. I can't even save myself, thought Sebastian, and he felt tears well in his eyes. They trickled down cheeks caked with blood. His head swooned as even this small fluid loss seemed to affect him disproportionally, as if he were wringing the final moisture from a sponge. A cold hand gripped his heart in fear, gave the tortured organ a painful squeeze, oozing blood from holes and tears in his body. A long, low wheeze escaped his lips, as if he were a stepped on set of bagpipes, and he heard the monster grunt and snuffle in response.

Suddenly, light burst over Sebastian and he was tumbling downwards, part of a cascade of flesh dumped on the ground. His fall was cushioned by the corpses, and he made no sound. He could see nothing now except a brilliant ball of light, and he wondered if he was already dead, the golden gates of heaven opening up before him.

But I don't even believe in God.

Perhaps this was the golden tunnel his grandfather had spoken about describing his near-death experience.

My pain seems to have gone away. Maybe I am dead.

The light pierced him like a blade, its beam penetrating his eyes and illuminating his skull like sparkling crystal. He realised what he was looking at in a moment of dawning horror.

It was the sun.

He was still in the land of the living. He was still in hell. A field of gore-drenched corpses stretched out around him, forming a wide inverted mound, a bowl made of flesh and bones. It stank, a sweet, ripe stench which stung as he inhaled and made him want to vomit. And his pain wasn't gone, only numbed by shock, his body a fragile tangle of broken pieces which ground against each other, the sensations just as tangled, feeling more like fingernails down a chalkboard than an actual physical torment.

It's all in my mind now, he thought, and he felt himself drifting away on a terrible sea, one filled with bloated dead bodies. They floated all around him, lifted up and dropped by waves. Sebastian squinted. The waves were brown, and they resolved into shapes—the giant hands of the monster. They swept through the bodies as if sorting them. With measured care, the monster selected one corpse and then another, picking them up. It shuffled over to another spot, placing them down in neat rows like a bricklayer constructing a wall. Frowning in confusion, Sebastian's face mirrored that of the terrifying beast, which was frowning in concentration, focused on its task. It was using the bodies to add to the rim of the huge, macabre bowl of flesh.

Almost like a bird making its nest, thought Sebastian in a detached fashion, as if watching the whole scene from the outside. He continued to feel divorced from reality as the monster clambered over the dead towards him. It paused and loomed over him, blotting out the sun. Sebastian felt the cold judgement of the Grim Reaper descend upon him, a hand stretched out to take his life. He put up no resistance as it picked him, as well as his mother, and lifted them up, one in each monstrous hand. Gravity tugged at Sebastian's devastated body and the pain rushed back in, smashing down his brain's defences and overwhelming him. He squealed in torment, but the beast took no notice as it clambered across the structure it was building and found a suitable place for the next two pieces in its grotesque puzzle.

It threw Akela's body over its shoulder like a dishcloth not in use, and, taking Sebastian in both hands, it twisted and pulled at his bent limbs. They extended with brittle snaps, and his lungs found expression at last. The scream was a high, descending wail of mortal agony. But the monster wasn't killing him, merely moulding him into the desired shape. When it was satisfied his body would fit the gap in the corpse wall, it plonked him down, gore oozing like wet mortar.

Sebastian whimpered, wishing the end would come. He had to watch as the monster squished and kneaded his mother's body to shape, working her already shattered corpse like an accordion. With a smile of triumph which was almost human, the monster slapped Akela's body down on top of Sebastian. Her weight pressed down on him as the monster went to fetch more bodies. These were used to extend the wall of flesh and build it up vertically. And as the weight of dead bodies pressed down harder and harder on top of him, Sebastian felt the life being squeezed from his lungs. Corpse by corpse, the sun was blotted out and access to air cut off. His mother's butchered carcass smothered him, and he suffocated in her deathly embrace.

There was no bright light, only eternal darkness.

23

Conrad had been playing chess in the park when he got the call. He recognised the number, and it was important, but he let them wait, keeping the caller dangling on the hook the same as he did his opponent, leading them on, letting them get him in check over and over, only to suddenly and unexpectedly thwart their plans, destroy their hopes of victory and reward. To him, this made the game much more exciting than the money on the line. It was the real prize.

The phone kept ringing. He sighed.

"Will you excuse me?" he said, and slashed his bishop diagonally across the board like the strike of an assassin's dagger. "Checkmate." He placed the bishop down in its square, the dagger thrust into the heart with a precision blow to take the life of his opponent. They slumped in their seat as if they had themselves been mortally wounded.

It's not my fault if they play chess at stakes they can't afford to lose, thought Conrad with a vicious smile. He got up, not asking for his winnings in cash. Instead he stood there, looming like a debt collector as his opponent took out his own phone, transferred the crypto currency. Only once he heard the bright tone on his device did the true dopamine release occur, and Conrad shuddered with pleasure.

The only pleasure I have left, the exchange of life for money, he thought, looking at the man across the board from him, aware that if he'd not paid up he was willing to extract payment another way.

A pound of flesh, a pint of blood—I'm in the business after all.

But his business wasn't death. It was life.

And that was why he answered the call.

***

On the phone was a woman named Wright, a park ranger in the Nightcap National Park. He listened to her patiently and—

despite being aware she was a bit too fond of the drink— took her seriously, because she said the magic word.

Bigfoot.

It was a word which sparkled in Conrad's mind, lit his brain up in ways few other things could. It wasn't only the promises of riches it contained. His life's work lay embedded in this one word—his sole purpose and obsession was to capture and breed the bigfoot.

To this end he constantly scoured the dark web for clues and leads. He also curated a formidable network of contacts, a machine well-lubricated with money so that people were always willing to pick up the phone and give him a call when they saw the signs of the monstrous cryptid. Wright was one such contact, but others were spread all across the globe, in positions high and low. After all, everyone loved money.

These people were Conrad's eyes and ears, an extension of his body, and they were vital to his work. He didn't get out into the field much—most of his work took place in 'his compound—and when he did it was only because he'd been alerted to an opportunity such as this.

It would be easy to dismiss Wright. Her story had all the signs of a tall tale, the details overblown and exaggerated. Conrad knew she was doing this to make sure she got his interest, to ensure that he actually came, because only then would she get paid. He quickly grew tired of hearing her drone on—she was incredibly boring, as were all drunks—and cut to the chase. He only needed to know one thing, that there were signs of the bigfoot in her park.

And indeed there were.

Conrad was no neophyte in this matter. As the world's foremost expert on bigfoots—a title he'd awarded himself—he could extract the precious nuggets from Wright's blathering, hold them up to the light to see their shine. It was enough to get his attention, enough to drag him away from his chess and his laboratory with the frustrated attempts at cloning—both of himself and the bigfoot.

There was money to be made and bigfoots to capture. But he couldn't do it alone. He hung up on Wright, cutting her off mid-sentence. He had calls of his own to make.

***

There was a trope in stories and films which Conrad hated above all others. It was called 'getting the team together.' He despised the way the story had to pause for an inordinate amount of time while the main character recruited some ragtag batch of heroes, a montage of boring bastards being paraded before the spectator as if they could give a crap.

Oh, this one wears camo vests and has war paint on his face all the time. You can tell he's an expert shot with a bow, because we have to watch them shoot an apple off someone's head to win a barroom bet, thought Conrad with bitter disgust as he entered his laboratory. *Then the main character interrupts the victory celebrations after the predictable success of the shot with some version of 'I'm getting the band back together.' At which point Mister War Paint drops everything to join the team, and they head off together to find the next useless bastard they require for their heist or whatever.*

It was enough to make Conrad feel sick, though the queasiness which swarmed through his guts might be because of the sight which greeted him in the laboratory. He looked away, trying not to think about the failed abominations floating in the cloning vats. There would be plenty of time to try again when he got back—hopefully with a living bigfoot, so that he no longer had to try to make his own. He kept going, past the empty bigfoot enclosures with their artificial natural habitats. He gazed wistfully into these empty spaces, filled with longing. He'd sold all his stock, and while this made him an ultra-wealthy man, he was impatient for fresh conquests, fresh profits.

"Is that why I've resorted to playing God?" he asked himself. And it wasn't just the bigfoots he was referring to. The need for good help was the other reason he'd been attempting such foul alchemy. He only trusted himself. And this is why he'd been trying to replicate himself through cloning.

"You can't improve on perfection," he said with a dark chuckle. Subconsciously, he was aware he was not perfect, no one was. But he concealed this fact from himself. Other people, they also hid behind veils, obscured their intentions and their true selves. They were selfish creatures like him, sure to sell him down the river as quickly as he did them.

That's why he never got too attached to his team. Not personally, anyway. Their bond was money—money in exchange for temporary loyalty, and for expertise. Conrad could do everything himself, of course. He was a master of all the tasks required in bringing in the bigfoot. But he was just one man. He needed more bodies. He frowned in frustration as he thought of the ugly monstrosities in the vats, imperfect replicas he would have to destroy with cleansing fire.

One day I won't have to rely on redshirts such as these, he thought as he entered a briefing room. Seated around a giant table was the assorted array of bastards he required, the product of his phone calls. None wore a camo vest. Instead they dressed in the plain black fatigues of mercenaries, devoid of insignia. They had no war paint on their faces. Instead, they sported blank expressions, their eyes hard pieces of flint. These were some serious sons of bitches, killers one and all. They were just the kind of people he needed.

But they meant nothing to Conrad, their usefulness beginning and ending in their ability to aid and protect him as he went into the monster's lair and snatched away the most precious of commodities—a bigfoot capable of breeding more bigfoots.

24

The sun shone down on a never-ending nightmare as Victor stumbled into the clearing around the ranger's cabin, weary, dirty, and footsore. He'd led the Cub Scouts on a gruelling death march out of the wilderness, and they trailed behind him like a string of helpless ducklings. Their mewling cries of complaint and protest were lost in his ears like so much mindless quacking in the distance, and he couldn't be sure he'd not lost some of them along the way.

The bigfoot has already thinned their numbers. What difference is a few more now?

He cursed himself for this thinking. It wasn't very Christian of him. Yet he couldn't help but be numbed by tiredness, his cup of empathy drained by the ordeal of dragging the pack of helpless children out of the forest. He took a deep breath in and out, blinked to clear his thinking.

"What would Jesus do?" he asked himself. He did not have an answer, and he felt his faith failing him. He had tried to follow the example of Moses, lead a people shackled by fear and exhaustion out of their enslavement. He'd set them free, but the freedom led to more danger, the national park huge and wild. The kids couldn't look after themselves, and yet he couldn't help but feel he'd already done his part. Now he wanted to hand them over to Wright and go to sleep forever.

Surely her maternal instinct will kick in. She can't be so callous, not in the face of such obvious suffering.

He wasn't sure about this. And because he'd taken her liquor with him in the truck, it seemed much more probable she'd be in a bad mood and would be no help to him and the children.

You really are a shitty park ranger, Wright.

He swallowed a lump in his throat. It had the bitter taste of guilt.

I'm no better. I was too late to save most of the kids.

He shuddered, remembering the mangled corpse he'd held in his arm, the way it had come apart like a ragdoll with loose seams. The stench which rose up as it split open like an overripe fruit would haunt him for the rest of his days. He could still smell it now, emanating from the unwashed bodies of the Cubs as they shuffled in the dust like zombies. He looked at the holocaust survivor faces of the children, their eye sockets blackened with fatigue and sunken with horror. It was easy to imagine them dead as well.

And they are. Dead inside, that is. They'll remember this forever. It's imprinted itself on their souls. They'll never be free of it. Damn it all to hell, I'll *never be free of it. We'll be tied to this one memory for the rest of our lives, slaves to the horror. I have not led them out of harm's way. The harm will follow wherever they go. The bigfoot has ended their childhood as surely as it did for those it crushed with its heavy clubbed fists.*

Shaking his head in disgust, Victor felt his anger towards Wright building.

This is her fault. She could have called for help.

This feeling of betrayal at her negligence was heightened by the fact that all was quiet around the cabin. No one stirred through the windows. No cars were parked out front. Wright had done nothing, would do nothing, if she was even still there at all.

I don't blame her for running away. It's what I should have done.

He stepped up to the cabin. Despite it being his place of work and sometime home, he felt like a visitor, or trespasser, or at least a vagrant asking for help from an unlikely quarter. For this reason, he lifted his fist and knocked on the door, rather than fumbling with the door knob, forcing his way in on that quiet space which seemed to him hallowed ground. After he knocked, he took a step back, like a salesman waiting to make his pitch, seeking the approval and good will of those inside. It was a long time before the door opened in response.

It wasn't Wright who answered it, though, and yet the face was familiar. It took Victor a few seconds to place them, as they were out of their usual setting and thus their whole demeanour was altered.

"Arlo?" asked Victor, recognising the raver. "What are you doing here?"

***

Arlo was naked, and Victor shielded his eyes as if from the glare of the man's pale skin, which shone like porcelain in the sunlight.

"For God's sake, put some clothes on. There are children present," said Victor, using his other hand to wave vaguely back at the children, who ran around, clucking like excited chickens, seemingly brought back to life by the novelty of nudity.

Arlo squinted at Victor as if he were similarly too bright to look at directly. The sun was at Victor's back, and he cast a shadow which passed across Arlo's face. Victor's own head was an eclipse and the sun formed a fiery halo around it.

"Is that you, Jesus?" asked Arlo, reverently, but there was no warmth in the smile which broke on his face. It was the dull smile of an idiot relieved of his madness, happy to be walking towards the light at the end of the tunnel if only it would mean the cessation of the nightmare realm he'd experienced his whole life.

"What? No," said Victor. "Don't blaspheme."

"Sorry, I didn't mean to take your name in vain."

"I'm not Jesus, you simpleton. I'm the park ranger, John Victor. We've met before."

"Doesn't ring a bell. I've heard of Jesus though. You're sure you're not him?"

"I know my own name. And I'm damned sure I'm not Jesus!"

"I wouldn't have a clue what my name is," said Arlo vaguely, and he looked at his hands as if expecting it to be written on the palms. He started licking them.

"Get out of my way, you drugged out loser," said Victor. "Where's Wright?"

Arlo looked up. "Who?" he mumbled with his tongue still pressed against his palm.

Victor rolled his eyes. "Sophie."

"I'm here," said Wright, coming up behind Arlo and elbowing past him. She was also naked. Her huge breasts seemed to fill the doorway. Victor's eyes went wide. He'd seen them before, of course, but there was something about them being outside, exposed to the sunlight, with the trees all around, which added to the effect of those dazzling orbs. He didn't tell her to cover up.

"You're drooling, Victor," she said.

Victor self-consciously wiped his mouth. He hadn't been drooling. Instead, his hand came away smeared with blood. The sight of it brought back visions of visceral horrors he wanted to forget. Desperate for relief from the burden of those gore-soaked memories, he leaned forward to place his head upon the soft cushions of Wright's tits. She recoiled, her nipples stiffening in the mountain breeze to point at him accusingly.

"You stole the truck," she said.

Victor straightened. "It's my truck too. It's a work truck."

"I had a month's worth of booze in the back."

"It's gone."

She raised an eyebrow. "You drank all of it?"

"No, the truck got wrecked."

She winced, though whether she was more pained about the loss of the truck or the liquor wasn't clear.

"What's this loser doing here?" Victor asked, jerking his head at Arlo. The moron was still licking his hand like he intended to eat it.

Oh, God, thought Victor. In his mind he saw the severed hand of a child on the ground, a bloody bone protruding from the wrist. He could see the bigfoot picking it up, munching on it like a chicken drumstick. The munching sound filled his ears as he watched Wright's mouth moving, though he heard no words.

Victor frowned. "What?"

"I said he just showed up," said Wright. "That fucking bigfoot killed everyone in his camp."

Victor looked from her to Arlo and back again. Not only were they naked, but they stank of sex. "So, what, you decided to pass the time by fucking him?" he hissed quietly, casting a worried glance over his shoulder at the Cub Scouts. They were pointing at Wright's body and giggling.

At least they're not thinking about the bigfoot anymore, thought Victor.

"I had to keep him here somehow," said Wright. "He was going to go to the police."

"I'm not a narc," said Arlo, snapping out of his personal hallucinatory bubble.

Victor said, "I don't think he was going to the police, or anywhere for that matter."

"Okay," said Wright with a huff. "You got me, happy? He had drugs and alcohol and I was desperate. In fact, that's all he had on him when he stumbled out of the woods."

"I can see that," deadpanned Victor.

"Take it easy. The guy watched all his friends get slaughtered by a bigfoot."

"Oh, so you care all of a sudden?" snapped Victor. "What do you think happened to these kids?" He swept his arm around to indicate the huddled Cub Scouts. As if responding to the movement like a stage direction, the Cubs remembered their ordeal and started to cry, a heaving mass of tortured humanity wailing at the sky and rubbing their faces with dirty hands.

"I can guess," said Wright with a shrug.

"Guess? I was there, you callous bitch, and I can tell you for a fact, it was fucked up."

"Okay, I don't need a lecture about it."

"You're some piece of work," said Victor, giving her a shove. "You knew and you did nothing."

She swatted at his hand as if it were an annoying fly. "Don't touch me."

"Oh, your body is so sacred now, is it?"

She stuck out her chest, lifted her chin. "I do what I want."

"You don't have to tell me that. You're disgusting."

Wright deflated, his words finally popping the bubble of her self-esteem. Her chest caved inwards as her back bent forward like an old woman's. Her tits sagged like empty sacks, udders with their milk dried up. Victor stepped away, repulsed by them and revolted by the fact that he'd ever been attracted to her. Even Arlo shuffled backwards, as if finally seeing her for the desiccated hag she was, a rotten corpse he'd stuck his dick into and was now afraid he'd caught something.

"Uh," said Arlo, looking around for clothes and finding none. "I think I've got to be going."

"You're not going anywhere," said a voice which froze Arlo in place and chilled Victor's blood. "No one leaves this place…"

25

"Without showing me where the bigfoot is first," said the newcomer, finishing their sentence in the same icy tone, then breaking into a manic cackle. The barking laughter bounced around the clearing like shots fired, as full of menace and devoid of mirth as their words had been.

Startled, Victor spun to see a man standing close behind him. His face was like a stretched mask of taut skin, tugged up at the ears by a wolfish smile which split the lower half as if someone had drawn a knife across it. The laughter had cut off as abruptly as it began, though echoes of it bounced off the rocky mountain slopes, making the man seem like a grotesque ventriloquist dummy, his expression wooden and lifeless. The eyes were like dark pieces of obsidian, full of striations of colour and hidden complexities which were revealed as they caught the light in brooding flashes. They darted like a robot's between Victor, Wright, Arlo, and the gaggle of confused and scared children. The latter were being penned in by men in black fatigues with automatic weapons held across their chests.

"Who the hell are you?" demanded Victor.

The man's mouth snapped open as if on a hinge. "Conrad Cruz, at your service," he said with a stiff bow at the waist. Victor looked past him to the Cubs, some of whom were crying, and all were looking around with fear at the tall men blocking their escape.

"Hey, hey!" Victor called out to the men with weapons. "Those children are scared, stop that."

"Don't worry, they're perfectly safe," said Conrad.

Victor jammed a thumb into his chest. "I'm looking after them. I'm keeping them safe."

"I think we both know you're not capable of that."

Victor was floored by this statement, the guilt crowding in on his internal thoughts like so many armed men. It took him a few seconds to recover enough to speak, and when he did his voice was a feeble shadow of what it once was. It felt like he'd left the greater part of himself up at the campsite with the dead Cubs.

"But I saved them," he said, barely a whisper.

"No one saves anyone except themselves," said Conrad philosophically, turning up his too-perfect nose. Victor took exception to this. He'd risked his life, thrown himself into harm's way to protect these Cubs. He straightened, tilted his head down menacingly, and spoke down his own nose, which he thrust forward like a duellist's blade.

"And what are you doing here?" he asked.

"I called him," said Wright, stepping forward. She hadn't put any clothes on, and she eyed the armed men lasciviously, like a predator whose hunger had not been sated. Arlo seemed to fade back into the shadowy interior of the cabin, to shrivel into the tiny scrap of meat he was, barely a morsel tossed down a cavernous abyss of ravenous appetite. The armed men eyed Wright, but took little interest, and when she noticed this she also shrivelled up, like an old, used up crone.

"Go back inside, you slut," Victor tossed over his shoulder.

"As you can see, I've been invited across the threshold," said Conrad with another smile which did not reach his cold eyes. He had sharp little teeth which glinted in the sun.

"This is a national park," said Victor, tugging at his blood covered uniform to straighten it. "*My* national park, and right now you're trespassing. You can't bring weapons here. You don't have the permits."

"I think you'll find, in circumstances such as these, that weapons are their own permit. They allow me to go where I please and do as I will."

"You're very sure of yourself."

"Who else can we be sure of?"

Victor had no response to this. He felt alone, with no one he could rely on. There was only him, and he had to act.

"So you're this bigfoot breeder Wright mentioned?" he asked.

"Yes, that is my profession," said Conrad.

"What sort of ghoul expects someone to mail a human leg to them as proof of a bigfoot?"

Conrad's face distorted in distaste. "I told her that wasn't necessary."

"So where's the leg? I'm sure the family would like to bury the remains of their loved one."

"Lost in the mail?" suggested Conrad with a shrug.

"I'm going to the police," said Victor, moving to step past Conrad. The gun appeared as if from nowhere. Victor stared down its barrel, which seemed to fill his sight like a huge, black abyss. He felt his soul tumbling down it, lost forever in the moral ambiguity of this awful man. Here was a power greater than Victor. And if it wasn't stronger than his faith, it was stronger than his flesh. The mortal terror he'd felt up on the trail and in the Cub Scout campsite came flooding back. He began to shake involuntarily.

"Everyone into the cabin," said Conrad, gesturing towards the door with the pistol in his hand. The armed men corralled the crying children inside.

"What about my money?" said Wright's disembodied voice from the gloom within the cabin.

"You'll be paid when I get what I came for."

When the last of the Cubs disappeared inside, Victor turned to follow them, feeling claustrophobic and trapped. He feared the cabin for the prison it was. Inside, he would be helpless, removed from any action, merely waiting for an outcome, which, he realised, was most likely not a good one.

"Not you," said Conrad, stepping between Victor and the door, which one of the armed men slammed shut, turning to stand guard. "You're coming with us as a guide."

Suddenly, Victor's terror ramped up to a whole new level as he realised he was now trapped not inside, but outside with these psychopaths, as well as with the bigfoot.

26

"I should stay with the others," said Victor, his concern for the Cubs a way to mask how fearful he was for his own life.

"You know the forest," Conrad said simply.

"So does Wright. Take her and I'll stay with the children."

"She's not seen the bigfoot. You have."

"How do you know that?"

Conrad cocked an eyebrow, nodded at Victor's blood smeared uniform.

"Oh," said Victor. "Will you not let me at least change my clothes?" He took a step towards the cabin. The hired goon with the gun stepped in front of it to bar his passing.

"There's no time," said Conrad vacantly. Victor turned back to see the man staring at the blood as if he couldn't draw his eyes away. His gaze was glassy, and there was something excited and manic in it, subterranean desire hidden behind the waxy veneer of the man's face. A hint of a tongue appeared at the corner of his mouth, touching the tip of a tooth which bit his lip.

Victor wanted to protest, knew it was hopeless. He saw in Conrad the same inhuman lust for destruction and possession he'd seen in the eyes of the bigfoot. He slumped his shoulders, aware there was only one way this would end—in the bringing together of these two complementary forces of chaos and death.

"My name's Victor," he said.

Conrad seemed to snap out of his reverie, brought back to reality by the statement of a fact. "Yes, I know who you are."

"You do?"

"It's my job to know everything."

"And yet you don't know the park, don't know where the bigfoot is."

"I'm a man who knows how to hire specialist help when he needs it."

"I'm not your employee."

"All the same, you'll do what I say." Conrad jerked the pistol as if it were a hound sniffing the air, smelling Victor's fear. The gun seemed alive, barely restrained by its master. Victor knew how close he was to death, but found he didn't care much anymore. He was so tired, so fed up, and if he died, he at least wanted to go to heaven.

"I'm not going to show you the way," he said, stiffening his spine like a martyr tied to a stake.

"Don't you care about those kids?" asked Conrad.

"You know I do."

"Then surely you want me to remove the bigfoot from *your* park, right? That way it can't hurt anyone ever again. I'm performing a service, like when you remove a dangerous snake from the trail."

Victor scoffed at this, but he saw the sense in it all the same. He looked back at the cabin and saw the Cubs crowding at one of the windows, staring at him with forlorn eyes. He forced himself to look away. At least they were out of harm's way, but they needed caring for, medical treatment. And, what was worse to Victor and his Christian faith, they were locked up with Wright and Arlo and their degeneracy. It would taint them as surely as the blood staining Victor's clothes. He rubbed at a dark red patch on the hem of his shirt, doubting it would ever come clean.

"Lead us to the kill zone and I can track it from there," Conrad said reasonably.

Victor's lips curled with disgust. "Kill zone?"

"The bigfoot's hunting grounds."

Victor shook with outrage, but also with a quickly returning surge of uninvited fear. His mind flew across the landscape like a bird, the eye of his imagination hovering over the Cub Scout campsite. The blood, the spilt guts, the smashed skulls, the snapped bones, the smeared gore… it was too much. It should never have happened, not on his watch.

But I can prevent it happening again, he thought, the devil's advocate speaking to him from one shoulder.

At what cost? Your eternal salvation hangs by a thread. This wicked man seeks to sever it, said the angel of dogmatic conscience on the other.

Victor felt torn, dragged this way and that by forces stronger than himself. He knew he didn't have a choice.

"If I show you the way, you'll kill the bigfoot?" he asked.

"I don't want to kill anything, merely extract a valuable commodity into my custody," said Conrad.

"You brought guns."

Conrad laughed. "I'm not stupid. The beasts are dangerous."

"Beasts? There could be more than one?"

"Oh, yes, the bigfoot hibernates for years."

"What's that got to do with it?"

"They only emerge to mate," said Conrad breathlessly.

***

Victor shambled along the trail like a condemned man going to his execution. Trees lined the path, silent sentinels hemming him in, making sure he could not escape. He was too tired to maintain heightened fear, his body no longer shaking. But his mind was active, thoughts spinning uselessly around and around like shadows in Plato's cave, a parade of silhouettes masquerading as reality yet merely illusions cast by the glow of an unseen fire.

Is this all a dream? Maybe the bigfoot is nothing but the vengeance of God come to punish me for my sins, he thought, and the idea brought him to a halt. The barrel of Conrad's pistol jabbed in his back, goading him like a pitchfork. He turned around. Conrad gave a devil's grin, and Victor saw in it his own sins made manifest.

If the bigfoot has come to punish me, surely this man has come to tempt me further. He wants me to betray everything I stand for.

But as it was unclear to Victor what exactly he stood for, he said nothing, and thought that by perhaps merely standing his ground his actions would speak for him.

"Which way?" asked Conrad, his head swivelling left and right, leaving after images in Victor's exhausted sight so that he appeared to be a two-headed monster. "Come on, time is ticking," continued Conrad impatiently, waving his pistol around in a circle, the action resembling the moving hand of a clock. His hired goons fanned out in a circle, their guns pointing outwards like the spokes of a wheel, their actions robotic and machine-like. Cogs turned in Victor's mind, but the mechanisms were broken, and the teeth of the cogs didn't line up.

"Which way?" he asked, confused. He so desperately didn't want to have to make a choice, even though he knew he was set on a path, the choice already made, with a conclusion inevitable. Though what that conclusion was, he didn't know.

"To the campsite," said Conrad. His twin heads coalesced into a single one, though it continued to have two faces, each overlaid with the other, one annoyed and hungry for action, the other unemotional, distant, as if he were watching events unfold with cold detachment, uninvolved in the outcome.

"There are two," said Victor, his mouth feeling dry and his words a hoarse croak. He looked around, saw they were at a crossroads in the trail, a place familiar to him. There was a sign at the intersection, and he wondered why he was needed at all. "Two campsites," he said, pointing down each of the trails in turn.

"We want the one where the bigfoot hunted," said Conrad condescendingly, as if he were speaking to a child.

"I-it…" Victor spluttered like a misfiring engine. He didn't want to use the word *hunted*. "It… visited both campsites."

"So it doesn't matter which way we go?" Conrad seemed disappointed, like his pet monkey wasn't performing the way he'd hoped.

He's trying to put the burden of choice onto me, thought Victor. He felt a tug of war between his ears, the forces of his conscience on each shoulder having each grabbed one end of a long neuron, and they were pulling on it hard, only now neither felt right, both equally hopeless and possibly evil. Like a puppet with no clear direction, he went one way and then the other, and in the end, got nowhere.

"I'd prefer not to go back to the Scout camp," said Victor, the only thing guiding him the possibility of minimising future pain and trauma.

"And which way is that?" asked Conrad, looking up at the sign and frowning as if he couldn't read. But, of course, the sign said nothing about scouts, only the name of the campgrounds, with arrows pointing towards a terrible fate.

Victor lifted a trembling finger, pointed down one trail, and turned automatically to go the other way, fleeing from those awful memories of carnage, not thinking ahead to the other camp, where they would find novel scenes of slaughter, new horrors, and fresh tracks of blood and massacre to lead them onwards.

Towards the bigfoot, thought Victor. *All paths now lead to the bigfoot. I can't escape.*

"Wait up," said Conrad, tugging an invisible leash with a flick of his pistol. Victor turned back and saw the vicious grin on the man's face.

Conrad said, "We'll go to the scout camp."

"I'd rather not," replied Victor.

"You don't have a choice."

Victor slumped. The tug of war inside his head ended, one side having won, though he didn't know which. All that mattered was that his brains were forcefully pulled out through one ear, splashing messily on the ground. He looked down at the grey gloop, and a part of him was happy to be free of the burden of thought. Gone was the weight of responsibility, but with it, the chance at saving himself through action.

He felt sure he was going to hell. There he would burn in agony for all eternity just because he couldn't stand the pain of living any longer. It seemed unfair, and he cursed the extreme nature of his religion, wanting more nuance, more grey area in between. He saw the smoke rising on the horizon, a sign of the eternal fire which awaited him. It drifted above the trees, and he felt sure it was symbolic, a part of his exhausted hallucination, but he could smell it, and the familiarity of that smell sparked memories. Looking down at the ground he saw no grey matter there. He shook his head, felt the brains slosh around inside his skull, and with them returned some faculty. A single thought lit up like a burning beacon.

That smoke is coming from the direction of the park ranger cabin.

Then the thought guttered out like the feeble flame of a candle in a breeze, and he was left in darkness, pulled along by fate, pushed by the barrel of a gun.

27

A gunshot cracked the air, scattering the scavenging animals, then all was eerily silent as they approached. The bonfire no longer burned in the centre of the Cub Scout campsite. In the heap of ash and charcoal was the park ranger truck. It was a gutted, blackened shell, a corpse of all mankind's achievements brought low by a primordial force far more ancient and powerful. It seemed a fitting monument to the hubris of humanity. Victor felt sure it would be his tombstone, the site of his death.

It certainly was for plenty of others.

In the cold light of day the camp was a sorry place. Bodies and parts of bodies lay strewn across grass made slick with dry blood which stuck to the soles of his boots. The fallen tents covered some corpses in a semblance of respect, burial shrouds to give them dignity in death. The canvas flapped in the breeze, giving glimpses of the hidden horrors.

By the sheer quantity of the dead it was clear the bigfoot had not returned to collect the rest of its meal, though there were plenty of signs it had been here. Huge imprints in the soft earth showed how it had trampled about in its orgy of butchery, and those tracks led off into the treeline, a clear trail for Conrad to follow. Victor's work was done, and he was sure he would now be rewarded with a bullet. While the others inspected the footprints of the monster, Victor went to the spot where he had confronted it the night before.

Here is the high water mark of my courage, he thought. *My greatest achievement.*

Looking around at the bodies it didn't feel like much. But at least he'd made a stand, and through it, he'd saved lives, not the least important of which was his own. He shook his head sadly, consigned to fate but wishing he could have at least gone to heaven. Looking around, it seemed clear enough what hell would look like.

A shape in the grass caught his eye, and he went over to it, picking up the bear spray he'd used on the bigfoot. He gave it a shake.

Empty, just like me.

He dropped it, a useless husk, same as the bodies of the Cubs, their souls having departed. Now they were empty containers with no purpose other than to remind Victor of his mortality. The smoke he'd seen before drifted across the sky like the black cape of an ephemeral Grim Reaper come to take him away. He sat down and waited for the end.

"We've a clear line of bigfoot tracks," said Conrad, approaching him.

"So you're done with me, I suppose," said Victor in defeat.

"It headed into dense forest, up into the mountains. I need you to help us navigate that difficult terrain."

"Just follow the bigfoot tracks."

Conrad twitched the pistol up. "Come on, get up."

"You think I care anymore?" said Victor, getting up all the same, though he felt it was his choice, not a response to Conrad's command. "What are you going to do to me? Shoot me? As if I care anymore."

"There are worse ways to die than a bullet, John."

"Oh, yeah? Name one."

"Burning to death."

Victor shot a glance at the charred hulk of the truck, remembered the fear and pain of the flames when the bigfoot pushed it onto the fire with him in it. The memory sparked his imagination. Pieces fell into place. He looked up at the black smoke moving across the sky like a poisoned cloud, and in it he saw a shape, one which described a complex scene of misery and agony. He watched the drama unfold, sure he was no longer imagining it, but rather experiencing some type of psychic transference, an imprint of death stamped onto the world of the living. A yawning abyss of horror opened to consume him as the dreadful reality of the situation formed in his mind.

"You set fire to the cabin, didn't you?" he asked Conrad with a painful swallow, razor blades slicing up his words so they came out as a ragged sound like tearing cloth.

"One of my men did," said Conrad matter-of-factly.

"But you ordered it." Victor didn't want him to escape the responsibility over semantics.

"Yes." Conrad's voice betrayed no emotion.

"And the Cub Scouts, Wright, and Arlo, they were still inside?" Victor asked in a whisper, staring off into the distance, seeing nothing.

"No witnesses."

Victor made a croaking sound as if he'd been stabbed in the guts.

"You have to be practical about these things," said Conrad, as if this made sense of it.

Yes, you have to be practical, thought Victor, his mind turning to the only avenue he had left open to him. He looked at Conrad.

"You don't happen to have a drink on you by any chance?" he asked.

28

Victor wasn't so much buoyed by Dutch courage as wilful numbness, the liquor from the flask of one of Conrad's men doing its work. He didn't put up any resistance, dragged along by the situation even as he was the one who led the way through the dense forest and up onto the jagged rocks of the mountain. He begrudgingly had to hand it to Conrad and his team—they were excellent trackers. There were times when even Victor, with all his experience of wildlife and the park, lost sight of signs of the bigfoot, and the team had to cast about for fresh spoor, always finding some tiny trace of the beast to follow.

In the beginning, in the forest, it had been easy enough, as the bigfoot left a trail of destruction in its mad flight from Victor's bear spray. But as they progressed, the beast became cunning and its mark upon the Earth more tenuous. It seemed to slip through the terrain like a shadow, and yet Conrad's ability to find signs of its passing felt almost like voodoo at times.

When they reached the rocky outcrops of the mountain—where the trees spread out as if to give them a wide berth—things became more difficult still. There were no more snapped branches to follow like signposts, pointing the way, no more impressions in wet mud, with the imprints of toes to act as guiding arrows. Now they searched for dislodged rocks, the occasional drop of blood, guided by the eerie certainty that the way led up the mountain.

"It's getting dark," said Victor, the booze wearing off and his fear returning as the sun disappeared behind the mountain. The silhouette of the peak loomed over them like the monster itself, casting a baleful shadow upon his soul. He shuddered, realised it was cold, his liquid insulation no longer a barrier between him and the elements, no longer protecting him from reality with its warm numbing.

"You got any more in that flask?" he asked a man whose face was shrouded in shadow. He didn't appear as a person at all, merely a man-shaped monstrosity, waiting in the darkness to consume him.

Just like the bigfoot, thought Victor, a now-familiar terror creeping back into his bones, rattling them around in his flesh so that he could almost hear their macabre notes like the wind chimes of death.

The man shook his shadow head. The darkness in that bulbous shape seemed to slosh around like liquor in a bottle.

He's lying. He's holding out on me.

Victor's skin itched with need. Hairs on the back of his neck prickled with fear of facing the future sober, a prospect he dreaded more than the bigfoot.

"Darkness doesn't slow *us*," said Conrad mysteriously, and Victor looked over at him. He was nothing but a black outline now, the sun extinguished behind the horizon, the gloom gathering like a fog of war. There was a piercing whine, the sound of some device powering up. The failing light cast a glimmer off two round circles, huge eyes glaring forth from a black mass. Victor took a step back from the silhouette before him, his fear making it larger than it was. Its glassy eyes were inhuman, the cold stare of a killer.

"Night vision," said the silhouette using Conrad's voice. But Victor could not see Conrad's face anymore, could not confirm he was human. He did not feel human himself. He was a ragged mass of flesh, hanging like mouldy washing from the armature of his bones. He felt insubstantial, unable to support his own weight any longer. His animating force was at low ebb, gone with the sun.

He heard a low growl in the darkness.

The bigfoot has come at last, he thought.

There was no spike of panic, only a hollow feeling deep inside him, the monster feeding on his fear. The growl repeated, closer this time. He took a step away, but found he could not get away from it. It followed him like a whining dog, demanding one of his exposed bones with its tattered strands of flesh.

"I'm hungry," he said without thought, his subconscious instincts finally separating the sensation in his gut from his fear-maddened mind. Something slapped him in the face. It fell at his feet with a rustling sound. He bent down, picked up the object.

"What's this?" he asked, even though he could feel that it was some type of ration bar.

"Last meal," said Conrad and shot him in the stomach.

29

The sound of the shot was small—a silenced pistol. It had an even smaller impression on Conrad. To him it was nothing.

To Victor it was everything, his whole world—and his whole body with it—folding around that bullet.

Conrad watched the man crumble in the green patina of the night vision goggles. His face scrunched up in agony, and the yelp of surprise he made was more like a dog than a human. Then he started to whinge and wail. Conrad considered shooting him again, but he didn't. He was of no more use as a guide, but there was one more way Victor could serve him. He would live as long as he had usefulness. Such was the way with all those who crossed Conrad's path.

The park ranger was making a dreadful racket, but Conrad was content to let him howl like a wolf for all he was concerned.

In fact, he was counting on it.

Like the shadows they were, he and his men folded into the gathering night. And then they waited.

***

Victor writhed like a worm on a hook, pierced through by metal, his life hanging by a single, thin line. Like patient fishermen, Conrad and his men watched their bait dispassionately with their green glow eyes, and in turn, something watched them.

It needed no night vision goggles to see. The night was its natural habitat, just as the mountain and the forest was its natural habitat. Its brown fur blended seamlessly with the dirt, with the bark of the trees. Its form moulded to ape the boulders of the peak, and it was just as massive and immobile.

But the bigfoot had no intention to sit in wait this night. Men had intruded upon its home. The nest of slaughtered meat he'd crafted with such loving care lay over the next ridge.

And in it was his mate, giving birth to their child.

***

For Conrad, the first indication that something wasn't right was not movement, nor sound, but smell. It was the sickly sweet stench of death—one he knew well. As the breeze changed direction, the smell wafted across his nostrils like a fine bouquet. He sniffed it like a connoisseur, momentarily transported by the promise it held.

Then the hackles shot up on the back of his neck, and even his cold lizard blood flowed hot.

He spun on the spot, turning away from the trap he'd set, realising too late that he and his men were caught in a larger one themselves. They were as much the bait as Victor—warm bodies all, fresh meat for the slaughter.

An undulating roar broke the night. Conrad exalted even as his body flushed with terror—the bigfoot had come.

30

The monster broke free of the mountain like a huge boulder knocked loose by a rockslide. Gathering speed as it came, the great mass of muscle and hair swept down the mountainside like an avalanche. It charged towards its prey bellowing its great lungs out, massive footfalls shaking the earth. The sonic assault alone was enough to send even the bravest men fleeing in terror, yet Conrad's men, cool and professional, raised their weapons to fire. But even their sharpened reflexes were too slow for the gravity assisted assault of the bigfoot. It struck like lightning, blurring sight with its swiftness. It was a living battering ram, and nothing could withstand its awesome weight.

With a sick, meaty slap—a butcher's mallet tenderising a steak—the bigfoot barrelled into one of Conrad's men, turning him to jelly. He was thrown aside as if hit by a truck. His body flopped to the ground, a deflated sack of skin leaking fluids through great tears in the burst flesh. A second man met a similar fate, though one out of sight, as the bigfoot scooped him up in both of his massive fists and, lifting him high over its head, tossed the man screaming into a ravine. The crackle of breaking tree branches was punctuated with a thud, the scream terminated.

Conrad took a step back, eyes wide. He watched the scene of slaughter in ghostly green as the monster butchered his men. A karate chop of the bigfoot's cleaver-like hand broke a man's collar bone, continued downwards to bury itself deep in his torso, splitting him in half so that each side of his body flopped outwards like the sagging petals of a flower.

Another tried to run but was chased down in a few long strides of the bigfoot's massive legs. He was picked up, the embrace almost tender as he was smothered in a bear hug. The bigfoot stooped down, and Conrad had the impression it was going to kiss the man on the forehead. Instead, it opened its jaws wide. There was a flash of huge incisors like knives, spectral green in the night vision. With a chomp which made Conrad flinch, the bigfoot bit the man's head off, its teeth snapping closed like the jaws of a bear trap. Blood jetted up from the truncated stump of the man's neck, shooting into the bigfoot's face like a water fountain. It ignored this, chewing on the head like a man trying to eat an apple whole. The awful crunching sound could be heard even over the gunshots as the others retreated, pouring fire at a shadow which was no longer there, the bigfoot dropping its snack and moving like a strobe light blur, seeming to flicker in and out of reality. The bursts from automatic weapons were like the green tongues of a dragon, licking the night as they chased an impossible target. They blinded Conrad with their fiery intensity.

"Hold your fire," he snarled into his radio headset.

As the bursts died away, glowing afterimages tricked him into seeing the bigfoot everywhere. He spun around, trying to blink away the funhouse mirror visions of the monster and locate the actual beast. It took him precious seconds—ones in which he was helpless and could have been easily slain—to realise they were all phantoms. The bigfoot was gone, once more having merged into the scenery as quickly as it had first appeared. The only sound which remained was the pounding of Conrad's heart, heavy like a bass drum in his ears. Excitement mixed with terror, thrilling him in a way which made life worth living.

I could die happy... he thought wistfully.

But why die, when he could kill?

His blood was up, a familiar tug pulling at the root of his loins. He lifted his own weapon. He had not fired yet, as his first thought was to preserve life—there was profit to be had, after all.

But not in the bigfoot bull. He hadn't come for the bull. It was nothing but a destructive whirlwind, built to take life. He had no way of containing and transporting such a dangerous beast. It wasn't his target. A female bigfoot, though, that was another story, and, if there was one of those there could also be the most precious of prizes—a squin, a baby bigfoot.

His eyes lit up with dollar signs. He grinned with happy avarice.

I love what I do, he thought, as he stepped over the ruptured corpse of one of his men. The rest of them swarmed around him like faithful hunting hounds, gathered together for mutual protection. They were baying for the blood of their prey, warrior instincts roused and their thirst for vengeance for their fallen fellows unquenched. The barrels of their guns swept the ground like sniffing noses, seeking the quarry, unaware it had not fled, only withdrawn, a tactical retreat as it waited for them further up the mountain.

***

Victor kept quiet and watched them go, hoping they had forgotten him. It was only once they were out of sight that he moved, and in doing so he found his fear reversed. Their abandonment of him was a death sentence. He was helpless, alone, dying. Each movement he made was utter agony, every breath a battleground. He barely had any strength in his arms, and his legs would do little more than twitch pathetically when he told them to move. By the light of the moon he could see down the mountain to the forest.

If I can just reach the trees, he thought.

But then what? Those trees would mark his grave and his body would rot to fertilise their growth. He smiled wanly. Maybe this was all he could hope for. To become part of his beloved national park, forever.

He dragged himself towards the trees, those eternal watchmen who silently witnessed the rise and fall of mankind, and offered up his soul as the price to join their ranks.

***

Conrad led his team along a mountain pass. Their night vision goggles leant them confidence—no need to be afraid of the dark—yet still the night pressed in on them so that they were keenly aware death was close. Life balanced on a knife's edge as they traversed a thin spur of rock. To Conrad, this heightened state was what he lived for. He was running on pure adrenaline, immune to pain. He didn't even notice when one of his limbs was plucked off.

Hovering in the shadows like a spider, the bigfoot waited for them to pass along a dip alongside the spur. It reached down from an overhanging cliff, its arm like that of an extending crane. With the care of a surgeon, it gingerly and silently grasped the head of the man at the back of the formation and squeezed it like a grape, picking it from the vine, the string of men now one shorter, a limb Conrad no longer possessed. It did not respond when he sent it signals, the radio nerve endings lost in phantom messages. The rest of the men sounded off as he called them, but that one was gone, disappearing as if the man had fallen down a hole and no one had noticed.

Conrad paused the team with a raised fist, helicoptering the arm. They fanned out into a defensive circle, a radial of nerve endings spreading across the mountain's face, with Conrad, the brain, at the centre, feeding on the synaptic signals which pulsed in across the radio channel, status reports—all clear, all clear.

Conrad's brain was foggy, hazed over not with information, but from the lack of it. He felt blind, reaching into a darkness he thought he understood and had an affinity for. He adjusted his goggles, the mountain's rocks glimmering green like brilliant emeralds, a richness he sought to mine yet couldn't see beyond.

As he squinted, trying to make out shapes, two smaller gems detached from the mass of humongous crystalline rock. They hovered in the air, as if an invisible ghostly hand were lifting up this pair of precious jewels, offering them to him. They glittered with a promise of greatness, sparkling like stars in the night sky, their price beyond compare.

Because what man could pay that price? It was life itself, all of existence being offered even as the threat loomed that it would be stolen away. Nothing was permanent, every breath a loan from a greater force.

And here was that force, the power of nature manifest in those hard points of glittering light, shining in the darkness as they floated dreamily towards Conrad. He was lost in his lust for them, seeking to possess and control what was not his to have. This paralysis born of greed overwhelmed him until it was far too late. Only when they hung over his head did he realise the ghostly green corpse lights were not jewels for him to steal.

They were the eyes of the bigfoot.

31

Reality shattered around the barrel of a gun. It was not Conrad who fired, but one of his limbs, a man nearby acting without impulse from him, an automatic instinct to protect the brain, protect the paycheque.

Money still bought loyalty, still bought action. It still dealt death.

Conrad recoiled like a discharged weapon as the bigfoot's blood exploded in his face. The monster had taken a high-calibre round in its vulnerable stomach, and it stumbled forward, threatening to topple on Conrad like a felled tree.

But it wasn't down and out. The pain only enraged it, and it sought to destroy them before it died, if only to protect its mate and offspring. Conrad felt a thrill of delicious terror mingle with the avaricious desire to capture a squin. If he died trying he died doing what he loved.

But he had no intention of dying.

He pulled the trigger of his automatic rifle. More blood, more roaring defiance. Whether it was his own or the bigfoot's mattered little. Only one of them was leaving this place, only one taking possession of a newborn life. If there was a sacrifice to be made, Conrad was determined it would be the bigfoot on the altar, not himself.

So he rolled to the side as the monster threw its weight at him, and in doing so he nearly tumbled from a ledge he did not see. He kicked at the void, loosening rocks which disappeared into the dark abyss seeking to swallow him, a hidden ravine between rock spurs. Vertigo made his head spin as his night vision goggles detected no bottom, only the tips of trees, waiting down there like spikes to impale him. He let his gun hang from its strap and scrabbled desperately for purchase on the rocks as the bigfoot crashed down where he'd been a second before. A shockwave of skittering pebbles rippled out from the impact of the beast, and Conrad looked back, daring to hope it was over, that it was dead.

No such luck. The bigfoot wasn't done. It lifted its head and let out an exasperated snort, blood oozing from its wounds.

Conrad saw the frustrated rage in its eyes, the furious points of light pointed straight at him like lasers marking their target. It opened its mouth and spoke a non-verbal word which Conrad understood.

"Fuck," he said, mirroring the sentiment as the hot stink of the monster's breath brushed against his face. With it came a premonition of inevitable death, a curse placed on Conrad's soul. Time slowed, flowing like thick molasses in his veins, every beat of his heart heavy and painful. He inched his way backwards along the ledge, balanced on a precipice, every slight movement an agony of care as he tried not to disturb a single stone which might trigger an avalanche of bigfoot flesh.

All his care counted for nothing as a single loud gunshot ruptured the fragile glass of suspended time which seemed to have encased Conrad and the bigfoot. A stab of light like a fiery needle stabbed the beast in the arse, riling it to instant frenzy. It screamed in shock and pain, the sound slicing through Conrad's frayed nerves. Fear overwhelmed him, all sanity evaporating as he turned and ran, almost going over the ledge in his blind flight. He swayed and fought for balance like a tightrope walker as he fled along a spur of rock, desperate to escape.

The monster scrambled after him nimbly on all fours, hooting and barking like an enraged ape. More gunfire chased them both, kicking up dust around Conrad's feet and nearly sending him tumbling head over heels to fall to his death in the darkness below.

"Hold your fire," he said frantically into his headset. No response, the limbs had gone rogue, fear had severed the spine of the group. Now it was every man for himself, and they poured the fire in from all directions like the spokes of a fiery wheel. This confused the monster and saved Conrad's life as the bigfoot spun around and around, leaping between boulders to attack whoever was closest. It went after one man and then another, desperate for vengeance and blind to its own pain as gunfire blew chunks out of its flesh. Its huge arms worked up and down like crushing pistons, squashing men flat. They were like ants to it—small, nimble, fragile, numerous. Each one killed did not stop the mass of them from overwhelming the larger creature. They swarmed around it, their automatic weapons the biting stings to bring it down.

Tilting its head back to howl at the moon in impotent fury, the bigfoot extended its oversized hands to the sky as if to grasp it and bring it down upon the heads of all of its enemies at once. But it lacked the strength—blood flowed from dozens of wounds, its bones shattered by bullets, entrails hung out of its guts like the tattered flag of a defeated army. It slumped down on one knee, braced itself with a splayed hand missing two fingers, and tried one last time to rise. Its whole body shook with the effort and with the impact of bullets peppering its thick hide as the men unloaded yet another clip into it.

Conrad watched this noble, valiant effort from behind the cover of a boulder and felt nothing stir in him except outrage at his own humiliation. He did not like things defying him, and the fact he'd lost his head gnawed at his ego. The shock of adrenaline which coursed through him ceased to be the spike of a thrilling drug, instead it rattled his bones as if to remind him how close he'd come to realising his own mortality. The thought of dying was not something he relished. His mind shot back to the failed clones back in the laboratory. His legacy was not yet assured, but it would be. Straightening his jacket with a tug, he emerged from behind the boulder as if rising from his grave, determined to defy death, stare it in the face, and laugh.

He approached the bigfoot, a contemptuous sneer twisting his lips as it slumped over, dragged down by the weight of its wounds as if shackled by heavy chains.

Such a waste of valuable flesh, thought Conrad, calculating the price the creature would fetch on the black market. He shook his head in disappointment—a wild bull was no use to him, no use to anyone. If he'd raised such a specimen in captivity, then yes, it would realise that tremendous value. Out here, on the mountain, it was nothing but a stud which had outlived its purpose, a beast to be put down.

Conrad produced a stick of plastic explosives from a pouch, primed it with a radio detonator, pushing the metal pins into the soft flesh-like surface as if it were a voodoo doll. The bigfoot responded as if sympathetically linked to the artefact, its spine going stiff with pain. It growled and turned to face its oppressor, the movements of its shattered limbs sluggish and shaky. Yet defiance still glowed in its eyes. Those gems still gleamed, the bigfoot aware of its own value—something Conrad couldn't steal.

Conrad shrugged and tossed the plastic explosives at the bigfoot's feet as if it were a last meal, a chunk of meat thrown to a caged animal. It did not try to pick it up in curiosity, only sniffed at it with distaste crinkling its nostrils. It did not try to flee. Maybe it no longer physically could.

The humans, however, ran. They scuttled away like frightened insects, and only when they were a safe distance away did Conrad speak the word of power into his headset, sparking a blossoming explosion which lit the night and filled the air with a disembodied roar of destruction. Conrad's hearing topped out and became a single buzzing whine as his sight filled with a wall of dazzling green. When both died away, and reality returned, hazy through rattled senses, the bigfoot was gone, and with it the last obstacle between Conrad and his prize had been removed.

***

Victor heard the sound of the heavens opening, saw the great torrent of fire shoot up into the sky, and knew the world was ending—because for him it surely was. His strength was failing fast. He'd barely been able to drag himself to the edge of the forest. There he found a tree missing most of its branches. It had shed its leaves in the gathering cold of the season, and now it was nothing but bare wood, the remaining branches forming a crude cross if seen from the right angle. But that was the way Victor saw it, and thus was all that mattered—a cross, a final marker, a fitting place to die and meet his maker.

He propped himself up against the tree's trunk, spread his arms out to mirror the shape of the cross, and waited for the end to come as fiery embers wafted through the air, the echo of the explosion still reverberating around the mountain.

32

Conrad popped up from among the rocks like a prairie dog, swivelling his head side to side, his ears pricked to hear any sound.

We're close, he thought. *The bull wouldn't have confronted us head on unless we posed a direct threat to its mate. I just need to know which way. Would the bull try to get between us and its lair, or would it try to lead us away?*

He panned around like a radar dish trying to pick up a faint signal from a far away source, his eyes staring blankly into the green gloom, willing it to reveal its mysteries. A faint noise drifted on the breeze, wafting across his ears like a promise, the caress of a lover missing its other half. His head snapped to it, the bizarre and unique cry of a rare species, and it got clearer as the urgency of the calls increased. It was like the angry honking of a startled goose. He heard the distressed questions implied in its alien tongue.

Where are you? What is happening?

The female was scared, calling for the male. It had heard the explosion, a terrifying unknown sound like a question mark of uncertainty to punctuate its future. Now it was huddled away, vulnerable and whimpering. Conrad sniffed the air, could smell the fear scent like a delicate perfume. A smile split his face as a cold calm flowed through his veins.

"Switch to capture weapons," he ordered his team. His men pushed their rifles over their shoulders, letting them hang on straps. In their hands appeared projectile stun guns, canisters of bear spray, net launchers, and cattle prods which sparkled and zapped the air with a vicious crackling as they were given test jolts.

The honking returned louder and more insistent, as if the bigfoot were being goaded by the cattle prods. The inhuman calls were repeated over and over, but the panicked female got no reply from the dead male. Instead, its honking was answered by another sound—the mocking laughter of its mate's killer.

Conrad couldn't help himself. The joy of the hunt was upon him, victory felt certain, and so the laughter bubbled out of him. It was a joyous affirmation of his own life as he stepped over the dead, his path taking him up a ridge as if climbing the shoulder of a vast giant.

Even as he ceased laughing the sound remained, echoing around the mountain. The mood changed. He felt as if he was the one being mocked by this ancient edifice. His lips curled in distaste, not enjoying being made to feel small and insignificant. He kicked a rock with his boot. It was satisfying to shift this lump of the mountain, watch it tumble down, gather more rocks, leading to a landslide which rumbled away into the darkness.

Small actions, big results, he thought, gripping his net gun tightly in one hand. He chopped the air with the other, signalling his men to move out and surround the bigfoot's lair.

***

It wasn't a cave. Instead they came upon a nest constructed into a crevice between two spurs of rock and surrounded by a ring of trees. It was like a pagan temple, open to the air.

And full of human sacrifices.

The nest was not made of sticks or reeds, nor was it lined with soft grass and leaves. Instead, it was a giant bowl of flesh and gore, the bodies of men, women, and children stacked and woven together to form its base and walls, with bones jutting out like loose twigs. At its centre was the female bigfoot, her hairy body matted with dried blood. She was hunched over, eating meat directly from the structure of the nest. She ceased only to grunt a few panting breaths in and out, before returning to her feast, gathering her strength for the ordeal ahead. She was heavily pregnant—her distended belly a huge golden brown orb like an overfilled balloon ready to burst. Conrad felt a tremor of excitement run through his body as he saw all his dreams coming true. He urged his men forward with a click of his tongue into the microphone of his headset.

There was a crackle of breaking bones underfoot as they closed in. The bigfoot shot upright with a start and sniffed the air. Conrad saw her eyes go wide in shock, and then her face collapsed into grief. She knew her mate was dead. How else would these humans have gotten so close?

Conrad stepped forward and made a gesture like tightening a noose. His men emerged from the shadows of the trees. They were spaced out around the rim of the nest, cutting off all avenues of escape. The bigfoot started hooting and hollering, pounding the ground with her ape-like fists, her gore-smeared lips pulled back to reveal sharp incisors bared like daggers, threatening them not to come any closer.

For now, they didn't, Conrad holding his men back with a raised hand. They were like mastiffs straining on the leash, desperate to bring down their prey. They said nothing, their silent, blank faces terrifying to the bigfoot. The night vision goggles made them look even less human, like a swarm of insects waiting to feast. Their cattle prods probed like antennae, and the air crackled with tiny lightning bolts as they used these to scare the bigfoot back into the centre of the nest each time she made an attempt to break out.

There she spun on the spot, with no one to turn to, distressed and inconsolable, going into labour alone, surrounded by enemies, the sacred space of her nest tainted with intruders. Conrad would have felt something for her, but he knew nothing of motherhood. Despite the nature of his work as a breeder, he was not a creator, not truly. Instead he was a dark parody of a creative force, one who could not make, only steal what others made, claiming credit for the work of nature.

Even what he felt for his failed clones was nothing more than a selfish desire to replicate himself, rather than a wish to invite a new life lovingly into the world. They were a commodity, just as this bigfoot and its squin were commodities. They were something to use. He could never understand that here was a mother who feared not for herself, but for her baby, loving it even before it was born.

Conrad felt no love for his clones, only contempt at their failure to live up to his expectations. Did they not know they owed him everything? Yet they mocked him with their imperfection, a sure sign of their ingratitude.

And if they are the product of my DNA, replicated and reflected in the mirror of the future, does that mean I am not perfect either?

Conrad recoiled from this thought as the air charged with static electricity, portend of a momentous occasion. The moon shone down upon the nest, a concave bowl of glistening gore bouncing light inwards, focusing all upon the miracle at its centre. Conrad lifted his night vision goggles, wanting to witness this moment with his own eyes.

With an angry grunt of defiance, a huge chunk of human flesh grasped in her massive fist, the bigfoot fell flat on her back and spread her legs, grunting and panting. Sweat beaded on her inhuman face, heavy brows creased as she pushed. The birth progressed surprisingly quickly, the moonlight sparkling on the glistening moist orb which emerged from the cleft between her legs, the head of the squin like a shining golden egg. Conrad's eyes went wide, wet with tears. He saw something he could never create in his labs, something unrepeatable in sterile conditions. Only out here in the wild fury of nature was the act chaotic, primal, and pure.

The mother screamed, her whole body tensed, and the squin squeezed its way out, baptised in a wash of blood. It slopped onto the floor of human corpses, new life built on a foundation of the dead. Breathing heavily, her strength tapped by pain, the mother ignored the men gathered around her and tended to her newborn. She scooped it up, wiped its face clean with one hand and offered it a torn chunk of human flesh with the other. The squin nibbled at the meat experimentally, stuck out its tiny pink tongue. The mother's face melted into joy as she gave it a tender hug. The squin threw its head back and cried, sounding almost human.

Conrad felt his heart twist, wrung out by strong hands like a dirty sponge. In that tiny, mewling face he saw what he could never be—perfection.

But this did not mean he could not steal it for his own.

33

The removal of a squin from its mother was a delicate procedure. Conrad deployed his precision instruments in turn with all the skill of a surgeon. Though it was the safest option for himself and his team, he didn't dare pump the mother full of tranquilizers. While she didn't weigh nearly as much as the bull, she was still taller than a grown man and twice as massive. If she went slack and rolled on top of her baby, then all was lost, the newborn squished and worthless. The same could be said for the stun guns. They could only be used once she had released her precious bundle. The cattle prods were useful, however, and could be used to box her into an area, making it easy to shoot a net over the pair of bigfoots.

Conrad coordinated the attack from just behind the closing circle of his men as the mother tested their lines, her baby held close in the crook of an arm like a football. When she went one way, they would give ground, close in on the other side to tighten the ring, and sap her waning strength with painful jabs of the prods into her bulbous butt. She hooted like an angry chimpanzee, swung her free arm to fend off their crackling staves, clutching her baby protectively with the other. The men avoided her swinging fist, which she flailed about like a heavy mace, seeking to crush their skulls. But she was made clumsy and weak by the effort of giving birth, and while she was busy with one man it was easy to get at her sides and ram the prods up into her ribs. She would bark in agony and retreat.

Conrad had ordered the prods turned up to their maximum voltage, aware it would hurt as grievously as if they were running her through with a sword, only without lasting damage beyond a few searing burn marks. Unlike the bull, the object here was not to kill the mother, only to separate her from her young. Then she could be tagged with a tracking device and set loose. It was for the best. After this ordeal she would return to hibernation for a number of years to lick her wounds. With any luck there would be a time when she found another mate in the wild.

Then I can go straight to the source rather than suffer through this again, thought Conrad with a grim smile as the crackling light of the cattle prods lit up the face of the female bigfoot. Her features were of melted wax, hanging slack in confusion and grief, tears flowing freely on her cheeks, her mouth twisted downwards as if tugged by meat hooks.

"I've got you now," snarled Conrad.

The bigfoot must have heard his threatening tone, because her eyes snapped to him, and an angry snarl of her own rumbled up from her throat, a primal challenge, a mother protecting her young. She bared her teeth, flashing the viciously sharp incisors which could tear the jugular out of a man's neck. Conrad took an involuntary step back.

Sensing his weakness, the bigfoot hugged her child close and made a desperate rush at the ring of men, one final attempt to break the symbolic iron collar of mankind which hung heavy around her neck like a slave chain. She would be free or die trying.

Her charge was directed at Conrad, so he quickly sidestepped to put one of his henchmen between him and her. She kept coming, and the man was too slow bringing up his cattle prod. The bigfoot smashed into him like a wrecking ball, the man's bones snapping from the impact. He fell in a broken mess among the corpses of the nest, there to add to their rotting mass.

"Fucking hell, do I have to do everything myself?" cursed Conrad, digging his heels in, unwilling to give any more ground as he watched the enraged monster bearing down on him. He was the poised matador awaiting the exact moment to act. Time slowed, flowing like thick molasses. Conrad saw every detail of the bigfoot, every hair of its body. They waved golden brown and crimson red like a field of wheat splashed with blood. Beneath were the rippling muscles of nature's perfect specimen, grown strong and fat on human flesh. The face was a feral mask, a distorted monster from the primal heart of the jungle, but the eyes…

They were red laser beams fixated on him, marking the kill target.

Conrad smiled, his heart thrilling with the theatre of the moment as he stepped aside at the last second. She went charging past, missing him by inches like a bull through the matador's red cape. He deftly deployed the net launcher in his hand, aiming it into her path, and she ran into the net as if it were a giant spider's web. She was immediately tangled in its strands and dragged down by its weighted edges, tumbling to the ground.

Conrad's men ran in, hosing her down with bear spray and spearing her with the shooting prongs of their stun guns. She writhed and shrieked, a twitching mass of flesh, becoming ever more hopelessly entangled the more she struggled. There was no escape. Not for her.

But perhaps there could be for her baby.

With inhumanly fast reflexes, seeing the net spring open in her face, the bigfoot had released its precious bundle, hurling the squin over the heads of the men to land among the trees. Conrad had not seen the movement—he was too busy getting out of the way—though he did hear the cries of the small creature, and he turned to see it crouched under a tree, its tiny moist eyes lighting up with the shocks and flashes as the men took out their anger on its mother. They were using the prods again, turned up to their highest setting to exact vengeance in blood and pain.

"Stop that, you fools," said Conrad. They didn't listen, lost in their bloodlust, and he feared they would kill her. He looked again at the squin and was torn between the future and the present. The tiny bigfoot locked eyes with him, and fear darkened its innocent features as it saw his intentions. Conrad made his choice, only glancing back at the mother once, hoping she could be salvaged for his future, but aware one in the hand is worth two in the bush. He chased after the squin as it made a dash for freedom.

34

Victor was dying for a drink—literally dying, and the process was slow and painful. But it was not alcohol he craved. The horrible aching wound piercing his stomach had dehydrated him with blood loss, so if he could wish for anything, it would be a single sip of water—either that or a swift end to his suffering. He was more than ready to slip into the arms of death, the pain unbearable. It was as if he'd been pinned to the tree with giant nails and a spear rammed through his side. He no longer had the strength to lift his arms, couldn't move at all except to tilt his head towards a sparkling illumination which lit up the rocks further up the mountain. It was accompanied by a raucous commotion from over the next ridge. They were sounds he was now unfortunately all too familiar with—the enraged roars of a bigfoot mingling with the shouts and screams of people. It was a death struggle, a contest of strength and will, with life itself the prize. Victor was beyond all that now. Such things were for those who had anything left to lose—not least of all being their illusions. His were gone, ripped away from him like excess baggage he wouldn't need in the next life.

He sighed, his whole body slumping further, as if a knife had been driven into his guts and deflated the sack of air which was his body. He felt insubstantial, and the only thing tying him to the mortal realm was the horrible pain he suffered. It was the only thing he feared anymore. Not the bigfoot, and not Conrad. Those things couldn't make his agony any worse. In fact, they might end his misery with their mindless violence.

But he wouldn't be so lucky. They were gone. He was abandoned to his fate. And his fate was to sit here until death claimed him. Then he could rest in Jesus's arms, be lifted up to heaven. Or at least he hoped so. Had he done enough good in this life to balance the bad? He felt the weight of his sins flatten him further, so that it seemed his body was nothing but a thin veil drawn across reality, everything seen through this thin gauze, his sight hazy. He looked up at the moon. It was swathed in gossamer clouds, further blurring the lines between what was and what was not.

I saved those Cub Scouts. That has to count for something, he thought. But he hadn't, had he? They'd perished in the cabin fire, their bodies turning to insubstantial ash on the scales of his soul. On the other side were heavy weights—all his drinking, the sex, his laziness, his lack of will which let others continue doing evil through his complicity. He knew Jesus was meant to take on the burden of these sins. The power of grace would save him. But this seemed a cop out, and surely he would burn in hell the same as Wright burned in the cabin. Had she deserved that fate?

If she did, then I do as well.

He could feel the heat of hell already, a phantom sensation accompanied by a sulphur stench. His fear ramped back up, far worse than the mortal terror he'd felt when confronted with the bigfoot, because the promise of hell was pain everlasting. He bargained with his conscience, pleading for a way out.

I saved the Cubs. It doesn't matter that they died afterwards. I confronted the monster, and I got them out of there. It has to be something. It might be a single thing, but it has to be enough.

He saw movement across the rocks, a small shadow running before the moon's light as the clouds parted. His eyes snapped to it, but he no longer had the ability to move his head. He was paralysed by pain, crucified by fear.

The shadow was coming for him. It was death.

***

"Get back here, you little shit!" Conrad shouted after the squin. He stumbled and fell amongst the jagged rocks in his haste, slicing open his leg. He hissed in pain but otherwise ignored the injury. It was of no consequence, and he subconsciously filed it with the others he'd received in his blind rush to capture the precious baby bigfoot. There would be time later to nurse his wounds. Now, there was only the prize, so he got up and kept running.

His sight glittered through the night vision goggles, lit up with shades of green. But he was looking for a dark nugget of hair-covered flesh among these huge slabs of worthless emerald rock. It flashed like a photographic negative, an absence of light revealing its location as the squin made another dash.

Conrad was in awe. He knew bigfoots were not like human babies—they were not born helpless—though this one seemed a rare breed indeed, fast and agile.

Its parents were good stock, he thought, adrenaline pumping through his body as he chased after the black blur of hair. *But a squin still has limitations.*

Conrad smiled his predator's grin and picked up his pace, recklessly jumping from rock to rock, ignoring his pain. As long as he kept moving he could still catch it. The squin didn't know the terrain, or much of anything. And it was weaker than it might have been—he'd been lucky with his timing. Normally it and the mother would spend weeks gorging on the human flesh, completely consuming the meat nest the male had constructed for them. If he'd come across them after that fortifying feast, the squin would have torn him limb from limb, matching the strength of a grown chimpanzee. As it was, the tiny bigfoot had only two things going for it—fear and speed. As the squin darted nimbly over the line of the ridge, Conrad felt doubts creep into his mind.

It might be enough for it to get away.

* * *

The shadow which rushed down at Victor was the size and shape of a human child.

Oh, God, he thought, tears welling in his eyes. *One of the Cub Scouts survived.*

He tried to call out to them, but only managed a hoarse croak like a stepped-on toad. He wasn't asking for their help. In fact, he wanted to save *them*, as absurd as this was in his present condition.

If even a single child survives I might yet be redeemed and go to heaven.

Desperate for this deliverance, he made another attempt to speak, no words, just a grunt like a caveman. The child heard the sound and ran closer, and Victor felt his fear and pain melt into a mellow glow of peace. Somehow he gathered the strength to lift his limbs, hands outstretched to welcome the child into his arms. Once more he mirrored the cross of the tree, projecting this symbol of protection and grace across the rocks like a shadow cast by the moon's glow. The child ran towards its sanctuary, and Victor found he couldn't see clearly for the tears in his eyes.

Far too hard, the child fell against him, sending a jolt of agony through his guts and knocking the air painfully from his lungs. He wheezed like deflating bellows, and his arms snapped shut automatically like the jaws of a trap, holding the child tight. They snuggled close to him, making strange, whimpering sounds like a wounded animal, and Victor blinked away his tears to see better in the silver moonlight.

The child's face was close to his. But this was no human child. Staring back at him were the feral red eyes of a bigfoot.

35

Victor tried to recoil away, but all he could manage was to give up the effort of holding his arms around the creature. They fell like dead snakes by his side, and not even his terror panic would allow him to lift them again to defend himself. He fully expected the bigfoot to maul him, rip him limb from limb. It hardly seemed to matter that the bigfoot was much smaller than the one he'd encountered earlier. It was still a monster, its hairy arms clenched too tight around his wounded torso, squeezing the life from him. He grunted and wheezed, and, to his surprise, the pressure eased. The bigfoot smiled at him, its sharp little teeth glinting in the moonlight like silver needles. Victor grimaced, sure it was about to bite his face off. Its hair was matted with blood, caked with clumps of dried gore, undoubtedly from a previous victim. Here was nothing less than a red demon leering evilly before it devoured him.

Hell has come for me after all, thought Victor, and braced himself for even greater pain.

"Hello there," said a smooth voice like that of a sophisticated vampire sliding across the threshold, uninvited yet coming in anyway. "I see you've something of mine," it added, and there was a slight tearing sound in the words, as if all was not what it seemed, a trace of strain and effort evident, a fault revealed in a polished stone, ruining it.

Victor couldn't move his head towards the voice. And though he could still move his eyes, he didn't want to take these off the bigfoot. They were locked in with those burning red orbs, transfixed, and he felt that if he looked away some magic spell would be broken and the bigfoot would realise he was nothing but food and start eating his flesh. The nostrils of the bigfoot flared.

Oh, God, it can smell my blood, thought Victor. It pooled like hot piss in his lap, oozing from his bullet wound. The bigfoot cooed and fussed like a baby wanting the breast. It bobbed its head down, licked up some of the blood, and looked up at Victor again, a smile on its face, the teeth smeared red. It made a happy, bubbly sound, a baby burbling at the teat.

"You've a real way with children," said the voice, not unkindly, yet there was a breathless impatience in the words now, as if the owner was annoyed they weren't the centre of attention.

"I just wanted to save something," Victor said to the baby bigfoot, ignoring the shadow which loomed over him, blocking the moonlight.

"Well, you've saved me the effort of chasing this damned thing any further," said the voice from within the shadowy silhouette. Victor finally looked up and saw the predator's teeth grinning in a man-shaped outline, though they provoked no fear.

What more can be done to me now?

The shape bent down, arms outstretched as if offering Victor a hug. With the glow of the moon around the man, his head shone with a halo's light. For a second, Victor felt like he was being taken away, lifted up into the embrace of Jesus. But this wasn't Jesus. It was a dark reflection of that benevolent being, and all that was being taken away was the bigfoot, lifted off Victor, easing his burden. The shape straightened and the bigfoot howled.

"Thanks," said the voice. A sparkle of light, a dancing web of crackling illumination—a Taser disabled the bigfoot as it started to fight against its captor. Its body jolted and spasmed, went limp. Victor could smell singed hair.

"I hate to do that," said the voice with genuine regret, "but they're stronger than they look. It would have ripped my face off and used it as a plaything." The voice's owner turned into the moonlight, and Victor saw their face lit up. It was Conrad, of course. Who else could it be?

Victor felt like he'd been shot all over again, and he found he wanted the bigfoot back. It was only a baby, he could see that now, and that made all the difference. It was not the adult who had attacked him. Here was an innocent creature, something he could protect, if only he could lift his arms.

Then I could go to heaven in peace. I would have earned my place, he thought.

"What did you say?" asked Conrad.

Victor realised he must have said that out loud. "I want to go to heaven," he said, not to Conrad, but as a plea for mercy directed at Jesus. Each word wheezed out of him as if through the hole in his gut.

"I think you're much more likely to go to hell," said Conrad, lifting his head to look at something in the distance behind Victor.

"You're… the…" Victor said, panting with the effort.

"I'm the one who's going to hell?" Conrad finished for him. He laughed mirthlessly. "This Earth is hell. There's pain and suffering here, and it'll go on for all eternity."

"Give... me… the… child," Victor said slowly. But Conrad was already walking away, taking the bigfoot with him. Victor let his head droop and thought of hell. He could already smell the smoke.

36

Conrad returned to the nest and found what he'd expected to find. His men loitered guiltily over the female bigfoot ensnared in the mass of netting. She was dead.

Conrad sighed. He'd traded one life for another, going for the more valuable, but still grieved to see future profits wasted. He glared at the men, one after the other, made them shrivel like slugs under salt. He didn't say anything—they knew well enough that they'd fucked up. They also knew what type of man they served. Some type of retribution was coming. They flexed gloved hands nervously like gunslingers before a showdown. They had their weapons slung back in front of them, but none touched them... yet. All saw that he held the squin in his arms. It was their meal ticket as much as his, and so they couldn't afford to waste him and leave his corpse on this desolate mountain. He was the only one who could turn the bigfoot into cash.

"I'll call in the chopper," said Conrad after a tense silence, and spoke into his radio headset, ordering the extraction. The words took a weight off the backs of the men and they straightened. One stepped close to the dead bigfoot, looked down at it, then up at Conrad questioningly.

"Burn it," said Conrad. "Burn the whole nest, no evidence." If he couldn't save the female for future mating he could at least cover his tracks, throw rival breeders off the trail, not to mention the authorities, which were sure to soon come sniffing around, seeking an explanation. There was a lot to cover up, and only fire could do the trick. He glanced back down the mountain at the forest, saw again the vision of hell he'd seen when he'd talked to the ranger—the national park was on fire, the flames spreading from the cabin to consume vast swathes of the forest.

He tucked the squin tighter to his chest, watching the world burn. He'd got what he'd come for, that was all that mattered. Turning his back on the blaze, he sang a haunting lullaby, bouncing the squin in his arms like a sleeping baby, and took it further up the mountain, where there were only rocks, and the flames couldn't reach him.

He wasn't going to hell. He was escaping into the heavens. In the distance he could hear his deliverance like a whispered promise on the wind, the *wop wop wop* of the helicopter's rotors slicing the air. The craft was as yet unseen in the gloom of the night sky, but it was coming to carry him away, lift him above all this death and destruction.

Conrad's nostrils crinkled as the smell of roasted flesh wafted up to him. Below, the nest burned like a great funeral pyre, immolating the dead bigfoot as well as its mate's many human victims. Conrad thought nothing of the families of these dead people, of their desires to recover the remains, learn the fate of their loved ones, and gain some closure. The secrets were devoured by the blaze. His men stood around it like warriors who had lost their lord, watching the flames thoughtfully as their futures hung in the balance.

The helicopter swooped in over the mountain. It fanned the fire with its downdraft, sent the men scattering as the flames danced this way and that. They ran up the mountain to join Conrad on the jagged and desolate outcrop of rock where he awaited extraction. The helicopter came in close, hovering above them. None argued when Conrad stepped forward first as a rope and harness were dropped from the helicopter's open bay—he and the precious squin were the priority. One of them even helped Conrad into his harness, gave the thumbs up, and stepped back. Conrad tugged on the rope and shot skyward.

When he was safely inside the helicopter, and the squin strapped tightly into a bucket chair, Conrad turned to the man at the winch. He was about to lower the rope and harness again to extract the next man. Conrad shook his head. He spoke to the pilot through his headset.

"Let's get out of here."

***

Victor thought it was impossible for him to be in any more pain than he already was. But as the intensity of flickering red, orange, and yellow light grew around him, and the smoke closed in, he realised he was wrong—worse was looming. The bushfire came on fast, carried by a strong wind. He could only watch in horror as the flames rose up over him like a wave, and the trees either side burned, aware his flesh was next to be consumed in fire and pain. The smoke alone was unbearable, let alone the awful touch of the flames, which lashed out at him like demonic whips, welcoming him to the underworld, where all was burning sulphur and choking ash.

He spent his last moments in this hell, unable to crawl away as his clothes caught fire, searing the flesh beneath. He tried to scream, but could only cough as smoke rushed into his lungs. This was a final blessing, the only mercy he could pray for now, as he asphyxiated quickly, taking away the pain as his body burned.

37

"It's been years, and still no results!" cursed Conrad, staring at the array of screens in the control room of his compound. They curved around the walls, each with a different vision of the bigfoot enclosure, so that it looked like he was inside the multifaceted eye of an insect. He checked the tracker data, compared it to what he was seeing of the enclosure, and located Nightcap Alpha. The sullen adolescent was hiding among the bamboo again. Conrad's lips curled up in frustrated disgust.

I should burn down that stand of bamboo like I burned down your parents' damn forest!

Nightcap Alpha sulked as if he'd heard Conrad's thoughts, looking depressed.

"What have you got to be sad about? I've given you everything," said Conrad, and he had, from the perfect replica of the bigfoot's natural environment, to a varied, nutritious diet and expert medical care. "I even got you a mate, and what do you do with her? Not fuck her, no, not that."

He looked at the month's expenditure data on his tablet and made a pained face.

Instead you fuck me.

He leaned forward and tapped the bigfoot on the screen with his finger, as if this would goad it into activity. Instead, Nightcap Alpha sat like a lump, munching absently on a stalk of bamboo. Conrad considered going into the enclosure himself with a cattle prod, giving the bigfoot some real motivation, but for all his youth and lack of reproductive rigor, Nightcap Alpha was still a big boy.

He'd rip off my arms and munch on them for a while.

Conrad forced himself to take a deep breath and told himself he was investing in a tame bull, a prize stud, a bigfoot factory which prints money.

If I can just get the damned thing up and running.

The door behind Conrad clicked open. He didn't turn to look who it was. Only one other person had the code to unlock the door.

"What's our boy Alph up to?" asked Morgan, handing Conrad a mug of steaming coffee. He unbuttoned and shook out his lab coat, sat himself in the second seat in front of the screens.

"Don't call him that," snapped Conrad, glowering as he hunched his head down into his shoulders, sipping the boiling hot black sludge.

"I'm not going to say Nightcap Alpha every time," said Morgan.

"You're a scientist. You should be used to using the full and proper designations of things."

"Scientists have cute little pet names for their work all the time."

"This isn't a cute little pet, Morgan. It's a business," Conrad sneered out the side of his mouth.

Morgan raised his hands defensively. "Hey, don't snap at me, I just work here."

Conrad glanced at the man, then down at his expenditure data. One of the biggest drains on his finances was Morgan's salary.

How I'd like to cross that item off the list, he thought, but it wasn't a possibility, not yet. He still needed him—expert help was hard to find when it came to bigfoots.

"Doctor Morgan Bronowski," Conrad read from his tablet as if the man wasn't in the room with him. He tapped the name impatiently with his stylus. Morgan saw this and got jumpy, rattling off some of the latest figures on the cloning front. He made it sound impressive, but Conrad was no fool. They were as stymied in their progress to clone a bigfoot as they were in getting his captive pair to mate.

And the project to ensure my own immortality has yielded nothing but failed homunculi.

Conrad shook his head, a slight, irritated gesture as if warding off a fly. A bead of sweat ran down Morgan's brow.

"Helen's looking good," said the scientist, trying to change the subject. He leaned forward and manipulated the controls of the cameras in the enclosure, focusing on the female bigfoot.

"You mean Saint Helens Sigma?" said Conrad, watching her laze about on a pile of butchered horse meat and feeling less than impressed with her.

"Uh, yes. Her latest blood work is fine. She's eating normally. Stool samples show nothing untoward. Skin, hair, teeth, claws, eyes are all healthy—I couldn't be happier."

"That makes one of us then," grunted Conrad. Helen was the only item on his list which cost more than Morgan—her monthly repayments were killing him, but he couldn't afford to buy her outright. Not without cutting the fat on the budget elsewhere. He munched on his stylus thoughtfully, mirroring the action of Nightcap Alpha on the screen, who continued to chew on the bamboo.

"That's not good for your teeth," said Morgan with a nervous chuckle. Conrad stopped crunching the stylus and swivelled in his chair to face the scientist directly.

"*Alph* does it to sharpen his teeth," he said. "Maybe I do it for the same reason." He made an exaggerated motion with the stylus, as if dipping a freshly sharpened nib pen in a pot of ink. With a slash he used it to cross Morgan's name off his list, but he kept the tablet's screen hidden, held close against his chest like a poker player concealing their cards. He looked back up at Morgan, but he saw through him like he was no longer there. Something beyond had caught Conrad's eye. He got up with a start.

"What in the hell?" he said, taking a step towards one of the screens. Helen was still writhing on her bed of meat, but now she was clutching her stomach and retching violently. He spun on Morgan, his eyes like sharp needles, transfixing the scientist as if he were a bug on a specimen board. The man squirmed uncomfortably.

"I thought you said she's healthy!" spat Conrad, jabbing the stylus towards Morgan like a sword, who jolted in his chair as if he were being stabbed to death.

"She is! I mean…" Morgan looked at the screen in horror. "She was. I have all the data right here." He picked up his own tablet, held it up like a shield to ward off Conrad.

"Don't bullshit me with your data," said Conrad, slapping the device out of Morgan's hand. Its screen smashed on the floor. Conrad looked down at it, saw his own dark reflection fractured into many jagged pieces.

Everything is coming apart.

"Get in there and see what's wrong with her!" he barked.

Morgan quailed. "But she's not under sedation."

"We shoot her full of tranquilisers now and we could kill her," said Conrad.

And then there goes my deposit.

"What about Alph?" asked Morgan.

Conrad looked at the screens. Alph was docile, shy of the female. He wasn't coming out of the bamboo any time soon. "I'll keep an eye on him from here and let you know if he's on the move."

Morgan looked dubious, but Conrad jerked his head towards the door, his face a red mask of barely restrained fury. The scientist tucked his lab coat around himself protectively and scuttled out. A minute later he appeared on one of the screens, tentatively entering the enclosure with his medical bag.

"You better not let her die, you greedy bastard, or I'll use you to make a proper mating nest," Conrad said to the image of the scientist. He hoped it didn't come to that, because it was not like fertile females were readily available, even at the exorbitant price of the lease on this one. He snarled, once more thinking of the capital sunk into this venture, and with nothing yet to show for it.

I should have leased Nightcap Alpha out to stud, he thought, *at least then I'd be the one with the steady income rather than bleeding money.*

He shook his head, quickly corrected his thinking—there weren't enough other breeders to warrant one off payments as a glorified sperm donor. And that was if Nightcap Alpha could even be coaxed into breeding, something he seemed disinclined to do. Added to this was the fact his rivals would keep any offspring, cornering the market, and that would not do. Conrad was looking to the long game. There were buyers waiting. They were patient people who knew what they were getting—a collectible of the rarest kind—but this didn't mean they would wait forever. They could go to a competitor, few as they were. Worry creased his brows as he watched the female bigfoot go into convulsions, her limbs shaking, spit frothing in the corners of her mouth.

I need her to live, damn it.

He looked at the sulking male.

And for you to grow a pair of balls.

He ground his teeth in frustration. Morgan was advancing cautiously, edging forward and keeping his eyes peeled for the male. But the female was in a bad way. Her back arched violently, she spasmed once more, then went slack on the mound of rotting meat. Conrad cursed, touched an icon on his tablet to activate the loudspeakers in the enclosure.

"Fucking get in there, you mongrel! She's dying," he barked at Morgan, who jumped as if he'd been ambushed by Alph. He broke into a run, fleeing as if before the male, but one quick look at the screen showed Conrad that the male was staying put, going even deeper into the bamboo, still munching away on a long stalk.

When he looked back at the female, she was very still. What's more, Morgan had disappeared. Conrad searched the screens in panic, scanning the area around the female, but there was no sign of the scientist and his distinctive white lab coat.

"What the fuck?" breathed Conrad. He glanced back at the screen with the forest of bamboo, and could not see Nightcap Alpha anymore. The stands of tall stalks didn't stir. But the tablet showed the male's location, his tracking chip pinging red, showing he hadn't moved. Conrad's face crumpled in consternation, his heart pounding. He knew he had to go in there, but didn't want to, not with Alph awake.

If Helen dies, I'm finished.

This thought goaded him to action, got him up out of his seat and running to the door. He didn't care about Morgan's safety or what had happened to him, only that the man wasn't doing his job. Yet a twinge of fear prickled at the back of Conrad's neck, sparked by the mystery of the scientist's disappearance from the screens.

He probably pissed his pants and ran away. But I need the equipment in his bag, so where is it? He's really put me in it now.

Conrad would make him suffer for that. His anger spurred him further, and he picked up a cattle prod on the way, determined to use it on someone. Its tip crackled malevolently as he reflexively squeezed his finger on the activation stud, the sparkling light dancing across his face.

Someone's going to pay. And it won't be me.

38

There was an eerie calm in the enclosure as Conrad keyed the code on the door and entered. The juxtaposition of this to his mad rush pulled him up, and his run slowed to a trot, then a walk. He looked around at the artificial imitation of nature, the faint breeze of the air ducts stirring the leaves in the trees. The sound of it was serene and peaceful, and it distracted him, so that he missed the fact that the door behind him didn't slide shut with a hushed wheeze. He swallowed hard, reminded himself he was in danger, and pulled his emotions into check. He had to keep his wits about him.

He tucked the cattle prod under one arm, tapped the screen of his tablet. The trackers showed Alph still in the bamboo on the far side of the enclosure and Helen where he expected her to be, in the centre at the feeding and sleeping area. He slid the tablet into a voluminous thigh pocket, held the cattle prod two handed like a spear, ready for action.

He advanced down a path lined with trees, and felt eyes on him.

"Morgan, is that you?" he called out, head on a swivel. No answer except for the swish of leaves. He kept going.

The path led to a central clearing. Conrad paused at the edge, took a series of deep breaths to steady his nerves. The clearing was big, and he felt exposed entering that open space, as if there were unseen attackers among the surrounding trees, waiting for him to reveal himself.

"You're being ridiculous," he said, yet he got the tablet out, checked that Nightcap Alpha hadn't moved. The flashing red blip was still on the far side of the enclosure, the bigfoot hidden deep amongst the bamboo. Even so, Conrad suddenly wished he'd brought more than a cattle prod.

And see all my profits destroyed in a rain of bullets?

He saw those profits in tatters anyway, the still form of Saint Helen Sigma up ahead. She lay atop of her mound of meat, which jutted up out of the centre of the open space like a burial cairn. A scattering of leaves surrounded the rotting, stinking heap, completely covering the ground of the clearing—except in one spot.

There was a blank, black hole of nothingness in front of the mound. Conrad approached it cautiously yet with burning curiosity. It was a pit. He'd never seen it before, and it wasn't supposed to be there. There were thin shoots of young bamboo scattered about around its edges and something clicked in his subconscious. The pit lay between him and Helen, and he edged towards it with mounting dread. The hairs on his neck stood up on end as he reached the hole in the ground, a forewarning of what was coming. He looked down into its depths.

His lip curled in distaste at what he saw. Morgan lay at the bottom of the pit, his body pierced through with sharpened stakes of bamboo, their tips glistening red, pointing upwards at Conrad like accusing fingers, blaming him for this grisly end. Morgan's eyes were as glassy as those of a dead fish, and Conrad saw tiny reflections of himself in them—a vision of a fate which awaited him.

He snarled like a beast, not accepting this prognostication. He gripped his fist tight, his finger activating the cattle prod. He skirted around the pit, rammed the tip of the prod into Helen's prone form. He was unsurprised when her eyes snapped open and she sprung to her feet—she wasn't dead at all, only faking. The yellow tracking tag dangled from her left ear like an ostentatious piece of jewellery as she howled and danced about. She quickly shook off the shock, though, and turned on him. She swung her arms threateningly, yet backed away from the advancing jabs of his cattle prod as he stumbled across the mound of butchered horse meat.

"I'll torture you to the edge of your life," he hissed, lunging with the prod as if it were a sword. She darted out of the way and then skipped back in close, grabbing at the extended weapon, but ran away howling as it nipped her hand with a painful jolt. Conrad laughed. He heard a pounding, slapping sound, and for a second he thought it was his own heart beating and his lungs flapping in the breeze of his excited breathing. It was only at the last second did Conrad realise these were phantoms. Helen must have seen the dawning realisation on his face, as she made a desperate effort, jumping up and down, hooting like a mad monkey.

Conrad grimaced and shook his head—he was being distracted. He spun on the spot, holding the prod before his torso to ward off the attack as Nightcap Alpha charged. The monstrous creature roared as their eyes locked, Conrad's pupils constricting in horror and the bigfoot's expanding like red embers in a stoked fire.

There was a wet, sucking sound like a boot being dragged from cloying mud. Conrad grunted. He wanted to scream but found he couldn't. The weight of the bigfoot barrelled into him, bore him over. He slid down the slick mound of meat with a sharpened bamboo stake thrust through his torso. The monster's howling face was close to his, and Conrad saw that Alph's left ear was torn and bleeding, the tracker absent. He felt deafened by the shrieking of the beast so close to his ears, but the sharp pain of this was nothing compared to the agony as Alph opened his jaws wide and bit into his face with a sickening chomp of teeth on bone.

Muffled struggling sounds—Conrad's last words were incoherent as his face was ripped from his skull, exposing white bone. His tongue flapped in a gory void, blood gurgling in his throat. Alph chewed on the ragged scraps of nose and lips as he gripped his makeshift bamboo spear with strong hands, worrying it about in Conrad's sucking chest wound as if he were stirring soup with a giant spoon. Stars burst in Conrad's vision, red like the blood which flowed across his exposed eyeballs, the eyelids torn away and swallowed by the bigfoot.

Hovering over him, Helen howled in triumph, and got hold of the cattle prod. She didn't know how to use it, though she clearly wanted Conrad to have a taste of his own medicine. Gripping the handle depressed the activation stud and sparked the tip anyway. She cackled with triumph and rammed it into his head. Foamy red bubbles frothed on Conrad's lipless mouth, his teeth chattering as he spasmed.

Alph finally got his spear free, tearing it loose from Conrad's chest with an upwards spray of spurting blood, and immediately plunged it back down again, over and over. The bigfoot tossed his head back, grunting and barking as he revelled in the delicious slaughter. Vengeance was his, and what's more, his long dormant primal instincts found an outlet, savage, pent up forces unleashed.

Red turned to black in Conrad's mind as he went into shock and died, and Alph mounted Helen on the corpse, fucking in gore-drenched abandon.

***

Afterwards, Helen fell in a heap, exhausted and satiated, arms and legs akimbo. Her breathing calmed and she closed her eyes, curled up in a blood-spattered ball, and slept. Alph did not rest. He had work to do, his life's purpose finally activated, and he performed the tasks programmed into his DNA like ancient instructions carved into stone.

First, he retrieved Morgan's body from the pit. He used a bamboo shaft to skewer the man like a shish kebab and carried him to one side of the clearing. Then he did the same for Conrad's mangled remains, taking his corpse to the opposite edge of the space enclosed by the trees. The outer limits of the nest thus defined, and its first building blocks in place, Alph left Helen to sleep and slipped down the path towards the enclosure's exit. He stepped over the length of bamboo he'd slid into place to brace the door open when Conrad had entered, and he was finally free.

His whole life had been spent in that enclosure. Now he could move beyond its walls. He didn't want to leave, not permanently. It was his home, where he'd make a nest and raise his family, but he had work to do outside, humans to hunt, because only with their flesh could he secure his family's future.

Only with their deaths could he revel in the blood frenzy and live free.

Check out other great

Sea Monster Novels!

Robert J. Stava

NEPTUNES RECKONING

At the easternmost end of Long Island lies a seaside town known as Montauk. Ground Zero on the Eastern seaboard for all manner of conspiracy theories involving it's hidden Cold War military base, rumors of time-travel experiments and alien visitors... For renowned Naval historian William Vanek it's the where his grandfather's ship went down on a Top Secret mission during WWII code-named "Neptune's Reckoning". Together with Marine Biologist Daniel Cheung and disgraced French underwater explorer Arnaud Navarre, he's about to discover the truth behind the urban legends: a nightmare from beyond space and time that has been reawakened by global warming and toxic dumping, a nightmare the government tried to keep submerged. Neptune's Reckoning. Terror knows no depth

Bestselling collection

DEAD BAIT

A husband hell-bent on revenge hunts a Wereshark... A Russian mail order bride with a fishy secret... Crabs with a collective consciousness... A vampire who transforms into a Candiru... Zombie piranha...Bait that will have you crawling out of your skin and more. Drawing on horror, humor with a helping of dark fantasy and a touch of deviance, these 19 contemporary stories pay homage to the monsters that lurk in the murky waters of our imaginations. If you thought it was safe to go back in the water... Think Again!

Check out other great
Sea Monster Novels!

Michael Cole

MEGALODON VS COLOSSAL SNAKE

Brought to life by the miracle of DNA cloning, a 93-foot Megalodon shark has escaped captivity. With an insatiable appetite and unmatched aggression, it travels west for the Georgia coast, leaving a path of destruction in its wake. Bullets and harpoons can't penetrate it, steel nets can't hold it, and it's only a matter of time before the whole world finds out about it. In a race to stop the beast, the organization responsible recruit a marine biologist and a herpetologist to develop a plan to catch it. To do it, they must unleash the company's other genetically modified experiment—a 150-foot snake, resurrected from the DNA of the mighty Titanoboa. The pursuit leads to inevitable combat, and the scientists are forced to witness the deadly realities of genetic tampering. As the battle escalates, it is clear nobody is safe...and that nature never intended for these beasts to return. As the destruction mounts, and the death toll climbs, the true loser of Megalodon vs. Colossal Snake is humanity.

Tim Waggoner

TEETH OF THE SEA

They glide through dark waters, sleek and silent as death itself. Ancient predators with only two desires – to feed and reproduce. They've traveled to the resort island of Las Dagas to do both, and the guests make tempting meals. The humans are on land, though, out of reach. But the resort's main feature is an intricate canal system . . . . . . and it's starting to rain.

Check out other great

Sea Monster Novels!

Edward J. McFadden III

SHADOW OF THE ABYSS

Out of the past comes an immense horror. An ancient creature that must feed its voracious hunger. A massive landslide on Grand Bahama Bank sends a thirty-foot wave traveling at 150MPH toward the east coast of Florida, and the tsunami drags in something horrible from the depths of the Mid-Atlantic Ridge rift valley. Now a monster roams Florida's east coast and its shallows, searching for prey. Matthew "Splinter" Woods lives in Sailfish Haven. He's a washed-out Navy SEAL who lives off the grid on his dilapidated boat and has withdrawn from society rather than face his demons. But when his ex-girlfriend, charter boat captain Lenah Brisbee, comes to him for help, Splinter gets drawn into a battle that pits him against the strongest enemy he's ever faced as he races against time to find the monster before it turns the waters he loves blood red.

Eric S. Brown

PIRANHA

The rains came, flooding the sleepy, little town of Sylva. Sheriff Hanson never thought that he would be fighting a battle to survive against real life monsters. . .but with the waters came flesh eating, hungry creatures that swept through Sylva's streets like locusts, devouring everyone in their path.